Praise for Jean Echenoz

"Against a pungently evoked French landscape, figures both comical and grotesque move through a magic-lantern adventure story at a pace that keeps us turning the pages—though again and again we pause to savor the richness of Echenoz's startling, crystalline observations. Never a dull moment!"
—Lydia Davis

"Jean Echenoz has brilliantly exploited simple but little-recognized truths about detective writing. . . . Rarely has the difficult craft of story-telling been as well mastered as here."
—*Times Literary Supplement*

"A humanist rewriting Foucault with a satirist's wit, Echenoz deftly and amusingly meditates on who we are and what defines us."
—*Village Voice*

"Echenoz picks out the absurd nuances of pop culture and twists them into a contemporary detective book. . . . A hilarious read."
—*Publishers Weekly*

Chopin's Move

a novel by Jean Echenoz

TRANSLATED FROM THE FRENCH
BY MARK POLIZZOTTI

Dalkey Archive Press

Originally published in French as *Lac* by Éditions de Minuit, Paris, in 1989.
Copyright © 1989 by Éditions de Minuit
Translation copyright © 2004 by Mark Polizzotti
Cover art © 2003 by Ralph Gibson

First edition, 2004

Portions of this translation previously appeared in *Conjunctions*.

Cover and interior design by Mark Polizzotti
Fly emblem by Roger Gordy

Library of Congress Cataloging-in-Publication Data available

ISBN 1-56478-334-0

This translation was supported by a grant from the National Endowment for the Arts, a federal agency.
This publication was partially funded by a grant from the Illinois Arts Council, a state agency.

Dalkey Archive Press books are published by the Center for Book Culture, a nonprofit organization,
located at Milner Library, Illinois State University.

www.centerforbookculture.org

Printed on permanent/durable acid-free paper and bound in the United States of America

Chopin's Move

One

THE TELEPHONE might well have rung twice, but Vito knew he wouldn't answer. He put on his leg before pulling on his pants, as he did every morning when getting out of bed—in any case, no good news would ever be delivered by phone, and besides his leg came first.

The prosthesis was hardly new, and Vito Piranese had gotten used to it long ago: out of habit the straps slid automatically into the metal buckles, which had embossed black lines at the correct holes, perpendicular to the leather; under the shrieks of the telephone, these holes were impaled on their prongs. Vito guided them into the loops, counting what was now four rings. After five or six, he figured, most people hung up.

When ten or twelve rings had screeched through the narrow room, a tremor shook Vito Piranese's features, which then froze into a perplexed landscape. The telephone settled in for the count, took up all the space in the studio, which was too small for the both of them. The rings sliced through the air, overlapping, their reverberations holding together like hyphens—and by the time twenty-five of them had filed by, Vito understood who was calling.

Now it would never stop, so Vito took his time. He checked all the fasteners on his artificial limb, running his finger under the buckles and centering each strap in the hollow of its worn groove while thirty, then forty rings spewed out, bouncing against the wallpaper decorated with tacked-up photos of chesty blondes. At around the fiftieth, Vito Piranese stood up and walked without a limp to the phone, on the sideboard near the hot plate. From a drawer in the sideboard he took a ballpoint pen, whose tip he rested, ready for action, on a notepad; then he lifted the receiver to his ear and said, "Yes."

"Piranese?" went a voice.

It was the same female voice as the other times, with a soft precision that left no room for argument. Vito enjoyed picturing the owner of that voice, her no doubt imperious mood, her form surely like those of the women he had crucified on the wallpaper: long platinum blondes with wide scarlet mouths, ivory teeth, and tanned breasts to which one could yield without a second thought. So at the sound of his name, Vito repeated, "Yes. Yes, it's me."

"Thirteen, forty-seven, fourteen," said the voice. "Again?"

"Please," said Vito.

She said it once more. At the other end of the line there was, in fact, a tall young blonde, but she was sheathed in a strict tailored suit. She sat at a desk buried under telephones with different tones, some without dials, others loaded with buttons. To her right, at the bottom of a cabinet, slept several files, suspended like bats; and to her left shelves within easy reach held teletype machines, fax machines, and terminals. She hung up and turned toward a man who was also tall, standing near her in a midnight-blue suit, absent eye in dark face. For several minutes he had rested on the young woman a glance that was distracted, although filigreed with lust. "There," she said, "it's done."

"Good," said the man. "Now let him know I'm here."

Lifting another receiver, she announced Colonel Seck. "It's all right," she said. "He's expecting you."

The colonel walked toward a double door, knocked, passed without awaiting an answer into a much larger and longer room laterally decorated with landscapes, classical portraits of top-ranking civil servants, and exotic objects under glass: official gifts from foreign counterparts. At the other end of the room, a Charles the Tenth desk supported the elbows of a frail man hunched over a square of paper, a cigarette glued to his lip, one eye shut against the trail of smoke. There were no files on this desk, no books anywhere; only one black and one red pencil and the white square.

Motioning toward an armchair, the man then offered the colonel a pack of "Maryland"-style Gauloises, which had become a rare variety. These were cigarettes that one didn't see every day, that had to be special-ordered in tobacconist's shops, in short that no one smoked anymore except for this man, whose pearl-grey, slightly stained, and fairly baggy suit suggested a creature of the shadows who kept away from the grandstands and press organs, someone off-limits to the public. No one knew his name. Still, the fact that the Tobacco Authority continued to produce Maryland Gauloises for his exclusive use gave some small idea of his influence. He lit one with the butt of its predecessor. "No, thank you," the colonel declined. "I have my cigars."

"What's the situation?" worried Maryland.

"Things are falling into place," said Colonel Seck. "I just want to make sure Chopin hasn't gone anywhere. I'll know in a week and then we can move. We're off."

Two

So: 13, 47, and 14. Remembering the figures jotted on his note-pad was nothing for Vito Piranese: forty-seven was the year of his birth, everyone remembered thirteen, and fourteen came right after. He cremated this memorized data in the sink, scattered its ashes with the spray jet, then scoured the yellow and brown traces that adhered to the enamel. That done, he put on his pants, glanced at his watch, and looked for his bag.

Two hours later, Vito arrived at the Gare du Nord, which was coifed with a line of tall, pensive statues against the white sky, dressed in togas and supposedly representing various cities in which people freeze. Like the spattering of hotel stickers on a globe-trotting trunk, or as a lost letter returns covered in stamps, the word *Nord* was engraved all over the facade, in the middle of which, topping a cartouche indicating the train station's date of construction (1894), a clock also gave the time (12:36). Vito had to wait a moment across the street, at the bar called Au Rendezvous des Belges.

Following his instructions, at thirteen-hundred hours Vito then climbed into the number 47 bus, which linked the station with the Bicêtre fortress, getting ready for the exchange at the fourteenth stop. The bus was almost empty when he sat down in back to the left, next to the window and facing front. On the seat opposite him Vito placed his bag, a shoulder bag cut from crumpled, boiled material, the final state of leather before cardboard. Each time he'd had to use this bag, Vito wondered what poor, chilly, unloved creature, of fragile health and all-but-extinct species, had originally claimed such a material as its skin.

The 47 glided gently down Boulevard Magenta, then down Faubourg-Saint-Martin. Few people got off, still fewer got on: a retired hairdresser, a single mother, two students from the Cameroons. Under clear skies, in light traffic, the bus exuded the quiet ambiance of a photographic safari, this time of day being ideal for observing all kinds of wage earners let loose on the sidewalks to stalk their lunch, or sometimes to display their amorous wares. When the bus crossed the Seine, the sun in the middle of the March sky tried pallidly to reflect before being swallowed up.

The vehicle pulled to a halt at the foot of a cathedral. Vito donned shades that the Martian lighting in no way justified. With a sigh, the doors welcomed two new patrons: a young woman and a skinny old man. The woman said something while depositing her change that made the driver's smile explode gloriously, magnificent in the rearview mirrors; while the skinny old man, weighed down by a thin satchel, ventured into the middle of the aisle, clutching the slippery bars and the overly-high handles. Behind his ersatz Ray Bans, Vito Piranese watched him coming: mechanical and emaciated, his scarf and bifocals suggesting some former private school English teacher, extremely tired, no longer capable of anything. His satchel, evidently sewn in the early days of the truancy laws and now at the end of its tenure, could itself hold no more than very small things: light insurance and social security forms, prescriptions, or X-rays.

The old man collapsed to one side of the aisle, into the seat facing Piranese; he rested his satchel in front of him, his hand on his plexus, and panted. The back of his head smacked gently against the seat from the bus's ill-engaged start. Then he closed his eyes, his lips slightly twisted from facing against traffic.

After the old man had jerked his eyes open (the bus having braked hard at Banquier station), leapt up with a slight delay, and rushed toward the exit, Vito watched him cross the road toward the community clinic, the unloved-creatureskin shoulder bag hanging from his arm. Then he made the other man's satchel hop onto his knees, patting its secular leather all the way to Place d'Italie, where he dove into the metro. Returning home from there was long, but on a direct line.

Back in his studio in the Laumière neighborhood, Vito Piranese studied the satchel's contents. Typed, almond-green onionskin sheets indicated the first and last names (Chopin, Franck Eric Georges), address (Avenue des Ternes), and daily schedule of the subject he was to watch for one solid week, Piranese's task being to note any departure from this schedule. Two photos showed a relatively thin man with light-colored hair, dressed in a light colored suit, and apparently a bit younger than Piranese; one color photo specified yellow for the hair and pale yellow for the suit. One saw the aforementioned Franck Chopin at the wheel of a coupe or a shopping cart, against a backdrop of Baie des Anges or supermarket. Vito looked at these photos with envy, torment, and a sense of his unhappiness; but the following afternoon he was sitting on a bench in the Jardin des Plantes, not far from the main gate, waiting for the subject to show.

Piranese was a bit chilly, his body dry, his profile sharp. His black hair shone like a wig and his black eyes as if with fever. Sitting on his coccyx, his leg jutting stiffly from his torso, he glanced suspiciously at the sky, squeezing his fists into the pockets of a jacket that would be out of season for yet a few more weeks.

Before the one he was now practicing on this bench, Vito Piranese had held other professions: basketball coach up until his accident, then broker in nonferrous metals, traveling salesman before Martine's departure, and finally photograph retoucher. None of these had ever worked out except for one, the retoucher, when he'd done a favor for some discreet important persons: they had taken an interest in him. He'd had two interviews. Now, thanks to these persons whom he hadn't seen since, Vito regularly watched the people he was asked to watch, following the same protocol established once and for all: the interminable phone rings and the three numbers, the bus, the swapping of bags, never the same bus, always the same bags since the time of Mata Hari. Deriving from this employment just enough to live on, with an occasional movie, newspaper, or weekly television series into the bargain, Vito spent the rest of his life trying to forget Martine.

Of course, there had been the chauffeur's job that the important persons had vaguely promised him, but he envisioned it without much hope, given his leg. And thus without much compassion he pondered the sky, glancing briefly in other directions: to his right, a statue by Emmanuel Frémiet represented a bear in the process of shredding an Iron Age man; behind him, his car, a small, purple Ford automatic, huddled between two enormous royal blue Belgian double-decker tour buses; to his left, overhanging the doorway to the Natural History museum decorated with beasts and bushes, lobsters and lizards, a stone eagle gazed steadily at the Gare d'Austerlitz.

When the museum door opened to reveal the pale yellow suit,

Vito rose to precede the man contained therein toward the park exit. Leaving his laboratory, Chopin would pass by the Barbedienne bronze that depicted, in infinite repetition, Emmanuel Frémiet sculpting the homicidal bear, then would head toward his car—a pale, German, trimly designed Karmann Ghia coupe. From inside the compact Ford, Vito photographed Chopin entering his coupe; then he maneuvered into departure position.

The Karmann Ghia followed the river's left bank westward, tailed by the purple Ford, whose radio picked up only two or three stations on medium waves. While trying to tune it, Vito methodically recited Chopin's supposed schedule. He was calm and concentrated, although at a red light, as Chopin was getting ready to cross the Alma bridge, a song that Martine had liked suddenly brought tears to Vito's eyes, and on the other bank it was still raining.

Three

W<small>HEN IT RAINS</small> too hard on the Champs-Elysées, men who
have nothing better to do seek out a dry corner and wait for it to
pass. Their shelters are bus stops or shopping galleries, cinema lob-
bies, awnings. Several deluxe automobile firms have long been
established on the Champs-Elysées, and in the showrooms their
latest prototypes are parked, resting on new tires like wild beasts
sculpted in repose: exorbitantly expensive models that these men
with enough time to prowl around them, having sought refuge
there, can never afford.

Beneath the hoods, like opals in their cases, shimmer engine
blocks, twelve cylinders in a V, hydraulic lifters, and dual vertical downdraft carburetors. The men prowl in silence, afraid to
touch. If they are in twos or threes, they whisperingly compare
the options behind the laminated windshields; having opened an
audacious door, they don't dare close it. But these showrooms also
house elegant young fellows, devoted heart and soul to the head
office, whose main function is to joke with the dazzling hostesses
batting exhilarating eyelashes, then casually to shut any protrud-
ing door. The shutting sound produces a perfect chord, major and
lubricated, the way the keys of a new tenor saxophone sound in
the void; those prowling around the prototypes admire the sound
but feel no empathy for the young fellows.

From the Mercedes entrance it appears the rain has calmed, as outside people reappear by the dozens: hundreds of silhouettes, with thousands more that can be divined all around—among them the outline of Franck Chopin, still dressed in a light-colored suit hidden beneath his dark blue raincoat. Above him, in the heavy but clearing sky, two fat zinc clouds weigh like wineskins, from which several little pure-cotton fugitives seem to have escaped.

Chopin walked down the Champs-Elysées, heading from home with a small box in one of his raincoat pockets: a tiny cage of braided wire that housed a live fly. After the traffic circle, the avenue's arboricultural zone unrolled like a green carpet, bordered by wide sidewalks that were prolonged by public squares. On a bench in the first square, a girl sitting on a boy's lap laughed uproariously at who knows what; on the following benches, rows of temps downed silent yogurts. Indistinguishable among the silhouettes, Vito Piranese was not far away. He had been watching Chopin for a week: every evening at the same hour the telephone spluttered in his home, and Vito gave the tall blonde a detailed report of Chopin's day; each time there was no deviation from the predicted schedule. It was the last day of his surveillance and Vito was relieved—although it was always the same thing, you get attached to the client. Chopin continued walking toward Place de la Concorde. The sky finished wringing itself out.

From the sidewalk, the travelers from Wisconsin or Schleswig-Holstein had ventured out to the middle of the avenue: caught between opposing traffic flows, they photographed each other in the axis of the Arc de Triomphe, which limply waved its protective nets and giant flag in the distance. Near the Elysée Palace something like a brief official parade unfurled, raising a trail of whistles and sirens, sudden as the downpour had been, sweeping the blacktop clean by momentarily whisking the pedestrians back onto its banks. Chopin looked at everything: the women and cars that preoccupied him much of the time, the official parade.

Like the others, Chopin would also glance at the tenth young woman after the traffic circle walking up the avenue in his direction, the one protected from the fading storm by a multicolored acrylic scarf whose designs recapped an adventure of Tarzan's—but lo and behold that their glances, having crossed, held each other and did not move apart, became a single glance that enveloped them, warmed them, lasted. Chopin was moved: love at first sight, breath comes short and blood pressure goes haywire, ouch my heart is breaking, ay ay ay I am shattered. She passed by, more dazzling than the most explosive hostess from Maserati.

Since all of that had actually happened at the speed of light—this sort of glance can be highly charged and very penetrating— Chopin remained transfixed, without the slightest capacity for rational thought; and when he turned around she had vanished. So it would be in other circumstances that he'd meet Suzy Clair.

Three days later, a party at Bloch's, a fair number of people. Alongside the pale faces from the laboratory and their spouses were a few women, some not too bad but most not so good. The vast majority were unknown to Chopin, among them three who worked in advertising, two radiologists from Douai, a humanities professor at the Beaux-Arts, and two or three more Cameroonian students. On the green sofa, Chopin was consoling Bloch for having not been elected, yet another year, to the admissions committee—when he saw her again, standing near the champagne fountain, alone and dressed in something that was green like the sofa, with very padded shoulders and zipped diagonally.

"Still, it happens all the time with the union," Bloch sighed while torturing the filter off a Craven. "You remember the effect Fluchaire's motion had." But Chopin had risen, walked toward Suzy Clair without any particular plans, mind empty and heart tripled, mechanically repeating to himself that it happens all the time.

Although it could have been an icebreaker, no, they did not mention their glance on the Champs-Elysées: they started from zero. Wondered, just to see, how many mutual friends brought them together at Bloch's: zero. Exchanged names, a few notions of their lives, some idea of their possessions. Chopin stared excessively at Suzy Clair, leaving her eyes an instant for her shoulders and skipping by her chest toward her left ring finger, devoid of ring even though her possessions notably included, as she was just informing him, a husband who worked in Foreign Affairs and answered to the name of Oswald. Right. "With me," said Chopin, "it's flies."

As she smiled, he told her about some of the flies he studied for a living: the brown ones, reddish brown ones, red ones, orange ones, and violet ones; about the vitreous ones and the ferruginous ones with yellow knees and green or bright blue eyes; and about the more comical aspects of their behavior. And as she deigned to smile some more at his tie, which bore a minuscule embroidered elephant, nothing was simpler for Chopin than to evoke the habits of elephants, those who crossed the Alps or tromped on foot down Rue Saint-Denis; those whose tusks they used to carve in Dieppe when he was a teenager.

Suzy Clair's childhood, back when she was still Suzy Moreno, was spent in Blois. At present, Blois was no more than a small, overexposed, black-and-white memory, even though at a very young age Suzy had become the princess of the high-rises: nothing was decided without her say-so in the parking garages and sub-basements of housing developments, standing near the river or leaning over the pinball.

All this, of course, would not be told in one sitting, but via episodes with no particular chronology, in the course of three meetings that week. First Sunday at the movies, sitting motionless beside each other in the dark, brushed by sweeping colors and feverish violins. Then Thursday, at his place; immediately they embraced and admired each other, shivering in little ripples as if on the surface of water. But the following Sunday, in the Shakespeare garden of the Pré Catelan, Suzy stared at her nails and said that maybe they shouldn't see each other anymore. Right. "Well," said Chopin, "I don't believe that."

Not far away, like navy blue specters, stooped gardeners tended the bedside of the alley of Scottish moor that was supposed to evoke Macbeth. "So tell me," Chopin said gently, "what is it? Your husband?" She shrugged her shoulders and shook her head no. A pause, of which a blackbird took advantage to attempt an audition. Lowering his head, Chopin gave the young woman a once-over, checking himself in passing in the little diamonds of mirror attached to her ears. He lightly kicked at balls of briar, upset witches' shadows, while Suzy Clair told him what had become of Oswald.

Four

Oswald, when Suzy had first met him, had to his name only a black motorcycle, onto whose rear seat she had immediately climbed; then they had ridden throughout the city, almost throughout the night. The cold air brought tears to Oswald's eyes, which rolled along his temples and were lost between Suzy's lips as she pressed against him. Several drinks in an after-hours bar failed to dispel their salt taste, and several months later a son, Jim, was born. After three quick intramural changes of address, Oswald swapped the cycle for a station wagon; then they left the capital for the suburbs.

That was six years earlier, when Jim wasn't yet six months old. They'd found themselves in a new building, in the heart of a new town southwest of Paris. Foreign Affairs forced Oswald to be away fairly often, most of the time for two or three days in Geneva. Each time he stayed in the same hotel with interchangeable rooms and called Suzy as soon as he arrived; the next day he would write her a postcard, leaning on open binders overflowing with statistics, diagrams, and grids.

In the winters, his postcards written, Oswald would stare through the hotel window at the curb defined by a snow blower, watching the trolleys in outdated hues that rolled with a sound of felt. Everything seemed muffled, phonically insulated, as if the little school-age figures in bright parkas who covered the dirty white sidewalk had declared a plug war on the world's ears. The text on the back of the postcards was always short, private, generally affective (I'm kissing you in the same spot as Tuesday) or informative (the chambermaid could be Sophie's double), and the front depicted Lake Geneva in every season, or else the hotel facade with a pinprick in place of his window. These cards would almost always arrive after Oswald's return home.

Over the particularly harsh winter in which—double victory—Jim began walking and pronouncing the adverb No, Oswald had been called to the banks of the lake more often. During one of his absences, it had gotten so cold that the pipes and gutters had burst, the ice propping up the cornices with marbled caryatids fringed with stalactites; that time, no telephone calls or postcards arrived from Geneva. On his return, Oswald had announced that the trip had been his last, that he would no longer have to go to Switzerland. He had brought back for his bride two little compasses, fashioned into cuff links, that really told direction under curved glass. While Suzy had looked for a blouse so as to fix them immediately to her wrists, Oswald, staring out the window, had suggested they move. Now that the cycle of meetings in Geneva was over, he would have to show up more often at the Ministry; it might be a bit simpler to go back to Paris, and besides, "I've kind of had enough of this town, what do you think?"

Very soon they heard of an apartment, just the right size and exposure, in the north of Paris, on the metro line separating the bad part of the 17th arrondissement from the good. Streetside, their windows would overlook the wide depression in which trains came and went from the Gare Saint-Lazare, and the ones in back would open onto two small factories—one producing mirrors and the other making they'd never know what, but whose chimney permanently emitted a compact spindle of very white smoke.

Several days later, therefore, their plants and furniture found themselves sitting on the sidewalk, giving each other doubtful looks, nervous about this departure for the unknown. Then they were hoisted with the boxes of books and clothes into a forest-green truck, on whose flanks a light-green painted leopard connoted speed. To transport the more precious possessions—six paintings, twelve pieces of jewelry, an especially sensitive crystal service, and the cat—an upstairs neighbor named Jacqueline Monteil lent her car, an elementary Fiat that she seldom used. Suzy would act as scout, with Jim in the back of the Fiat lassoed into his baby seat. Oswald would join them once his file folders were packed in the station wagon.

All kinds of folders: with straps, elastics, or strings, rings or hooks, spiral-bound or clasped; a hole in the covers of some of them let you pull them out with one finger. Alphabetical and blue or tan, they had covered three walls of Oswald Clair's study up to the ceiling, sometimes towering in double-thick cliffs. Oswald had just stacked them, from A to D, in the front of the car, and hands on hips, he was now wondering if it would be the R's or just the W's that would keep the hatchback from closing. Suzy signaled to him with her lips as she started up; Jim waved a fist squeezed onto a one-legged doll. Oswald raised a preoccupied hand, with the smile of a distracted myope.

Suzy Clair, then, thought she was crossing the suburbs for the last time, skirting Créteil-Soleil before joining the beltway. Cords of Vincennes wood paraded by to her right; to her left were hec-toliters of Seine, then Marne. Jim had fallen asleep almost immediately. When Suzy twisted in her seat to check her son in the rearview mirror, the seat belt cutting a bit between her breasts, she remembered being in the back of the cream-and-maroon Aronde, on Sundays, when her fidgety parents went to take some air around Blois; she calculated that Jim would be four or five before he started asking if they were there yet every three minutes. An Austerlitz sun shone on Rue de Rome when Suzy parked the Fiat beside the grillwork fence bordering the railway trench. The truck was already waiting at the foot of the new home; the green leopard men came and went, each one under his object, banding together to carry the heavy pieces.

Having very little known family, Oswald boasted no furniture inheritance, and from Suzy's side came just a large willow chest from an uncle's butcher shop, promoted to the rank of bedside table: having known only the acid universe of sawdust, cold, and cutting slabs, with no prospects other than to contain blood-stained rags and knives its whole object-life long, this trunk was suddenly facing a warm and miraculous retirement, stuffed with comfortable winter clothing, furs and cashmere, angora, and now it was being carried on men's backs toward the heights of Rue de Rome. Except for this, then, Oswald and Suzy had bought all their furniture together, most of it conceived in the first third of the century. The copy of a Marcel Breuer chair, Eugene Schoen bookcase, or René Prou desk; a reissued Edouard-Wilfrid Burquet lamp: such was the Clairs' taste.

Suzy set Jim down in the largest room in the middle of the apartment, on a rolling device fenced in by blankets, in the company of stuffed toys and rubber objects; from there, the little boy could easily watch the movers at work. Then she wandered through the apartment. When the large biceps came to ask her politely where do you want this, ma'am, she smiled at them and raised her eyebrows, her shoulders. And when they were almost finished, she left the child with them for a moment, drooped in a placid arc over the walker, while she went out to get them some beer. She wandered through the neighborhood awhile before finding an open market, where a very young Arab girl tended the cash register. Suzy could have kissed her out of relief; then she returned home by another path. She walked quickly, straight ahead, glancing in every direction while hugging the six-pack in her arms.

Once the green leopards had been refreshed and dispersed toward their truck, hopping onto the seats and starting up as they whistled through their teeth, Suzy put two chairs at a table, installed Jim there with some magic markers, and began pacing around the apartment again. While inserting a cookie into his nose, Jim immediately began engraving the table's wax polish with the wrong end of the green marker. Suzy came by from time to time to borrow the red one, to sketch a project, jot down an idea for a room or the floor plan of the kitchen. Finally, it was only when the child manifested some impatience, scattering the pieces of an overly abstract puzzle, that she noticed she hadn't removed her coat. At that point, she began periodically checking the clock.

She had turned up the heat when they arrived, but the ambient air remained freshly moved-into, and the beginnings of radiated warmth sounded hollow amid the covers, boxes, and transient furniture. Suzy undid her coat, then Jim's jacket, which had been buttoned up to his ears. She plugged in the radio, turned it on, stayed for two seconds on two or three stations, switched it off. When evening came, she lit two lamps—a banal one and the Wagenfeld—then remembered the telephone the way one remembers a forgotten animal: the instrument was huddled against the darkest corner of one of the rooms, linked by its cord to the wall as, by its leash to a pole, an abandoned dog in summer.

Night had fallen, all lamps were lit; Jim had been fed and put to bed in a rough draft of his room. By now, Suzy was nowhere but on the telephone. She called in all directions: constantly at their old apartment, where no one answered; Jacqueline Monteil, who hadn't a clue; as well as her brother Joe, her friend Blanche, and even a fellow named Horst who'd more or less been her agent or her lover when Suzy had posed for the camera before meeting Oswald. She hesitated, then called the Ministry, but no one was there at this hour: just an orderly who didn't know anything and didn't want to. She remembered one of Oswald's colleagues whose wife had gotten incredibly drunk at the dinner celebrating the closing of the Vienna conference. She called them, but the colleague didn't know anything either; she could sense him alone in his room, dressed in his bathrobe, his wife at detox cure. It grew late and Suzy stopped telephoning, let the instrument take a breather. Perhaps Oswald was trying to call her.

When brother Joe arrived an hour later, Suzy was turning the yellow pages of a phone book without looking at them. To Joe befell the vain task of calling, all night long, the hospitals and police stations. As usual, Suzy slept poorly. The next day she called the Ministry and asked to speak to Oswald's secretary or assistant, his aide, a colleague, I don't know, somebody like that. She was transferred to someone who transferred her to someone else, went through half a dozen extensions, two or three of which were perpetually busy. In the final account, it seemed it was impossible to find anything like what she wanted in the entire network; but the police came of their own accord once Suzy had called the Ministry.

The police didn't seem very determined. They came to see Suzy, Suzy went to see them. In the days following they came back, she went back, it dragged on; no one found anything. Oswald had vanished without a trace, like a common pebble that falls into the ocean at night, with no one there to witness its imperceptible drop into the lapping of dark waters, its negligible splash in the turmoil. It was as if nothing had happened. And from that point on nothing would happen, except for a call from a garage mechanic in Villejuif one week after the move. The man explained that someone had left him a station wagon the week before, in front of the garage, with nothing in it except the keys and registration in an envelope in the glove compartment, plus money for a week's worth of storage and the number of a Mrs. Clair, Paris 17th, and what should he do with the car? Absolutely nothing more after that, and now six years had gone by.

Five

Having left the Shakespeare garden, they crossed the Bois de Boulogne. The Karmann Ghia rolled through the green shadows, the radio played Nat King Cole, and Suzy continued to talk about Oswald. So he was, just like Chopin, part of an organization in which people described phenomena, induced hypotheses, and discovered laws, except that Chopin dealt in the mores of flies and Clair in bloc politics. A man of tact and science, Chopin stayed attentive to everything Suzy had said about her husband, methodically, as if she were speaking about a new type of *Siphonaptera;* scrupulously he steeled himself against his conscience, so as not to wonder overtly why he should give a shit about this clown.

On Rue de Rome, the kid wasn't there—weekend in Blois—and Suzy offered to make tea. "After this, I won't say any more about it," she said. But she returned from the bedroom with a large flat box, which she opened: little identity photos floated on the surface of a bed of pictures.

Private pictures, marriage at the town hall of the 4th arrondissement—Suzy showed her father in the photograph, a dry little man with eyes glazed from forty-five years of skinning. Professional pictures, during a lecture or conference abroad: for example, at the Eisenstadt colloquium Oswald was in the upper right, between Professor Ilon Swarcz and the military attaché Asher Padeh; in the first row smiled the delegates Veber and Ghiglion. These pictures were somewhat jumbled, as Suzy often followed her husband when the colloquia were held in warm climates: in the margin of their days in Bogota, they could be seen squeezed behind a restaurant table, under the lens of a roving camera, Suzy blinking at a tropical flashbulb that was rudely reflected in Oswald's eyeglasses.

Whatever the photo, Oswald Clair never seemed very happy to be caught within its parameters; one always felt him twisting out of the frame, snared by what lay outside the visual field. At the very bottom of the flat box, a bilingual identity card established by the Canadian authorities for a trip to Vancouver offered a few details about his person (5 feet 9 inches, 139 pounds; distinguishing marks, scars, tattoos, deformities: none), with the simultaneous print of his ten fingers (if any prints are missing, conjectured a blue note, indicate the reason; if because of an amputation, it blushed, please give the date).

Soon afterward they went into Suzy's room, where they spoke no more of Oswald; then Suzy went back to the kitchen to finally make that tea. Still in the bedroom, Chopin listened to her bustling about in the distance, pizzicato of utensils and gargle of boiling water, while looking at the images on the walls: a seaport by Horace Vernet, a paragraph by Saul Steinberg tacked above the desk. And on the opposite wall, external daylight on sepia carpet, forty-three maharajas posed in 1925 for the Kapurthala jubilee. Color photography was just coming into use then: if not for several pale, primitive pinks and greens, a possible yellow, a so-called brown, one would almost have thought the photo was in black and white, as it hung over a large bed covered with a lemon-and-strawberry coverlet that was now all rumpled, wilted under the heat of bodies embracing.

Six

THE SUN on the morning after the morning after was exemplary: blocking onsets of depression, the anticyclone was working like a charm. Chopin had just chosen a patternless tie, lightly barred by a very fine blue line on grey. Once knotted, ready to go out, he made a detour via the kitchen, then via his hatchery.

The flies lived in a plexiglass case equipped with a thermostat, a thermometer, and a hygrometer. Inside the case, a glass cube contained pupae resting on a bed of sawdust, and inside another cube made of fine netting, the flights of hatched insects crossed paths. As two of them had in fact taken a fancy to each other, Chopin enjoyed studying a brief coitus under magnifying glass before tossing the happy couple a crumb of pork rind.

He was master of his time, accountable to no one for his work at the museum, expected to produce barely two or three articles per year. No schedule, because there was no woman in his life, because he was forever undecided—Carole always being too much of what Marianne would never be enough. In the elevator, a hand more decisive than Chopin's had inscribed *Nacera I love you* in large, feverish red letters near the numbered buttons, where their addressee could hardly miss them; they weren't signed, but Nacera would no doubt have a pretty good idea. Chopin pressed the lower button. Ground floor: the elevator gate, three steps, the glass door, the mailbox-edged foyer, and the main entrance.

The mail: usually a brochure or a bill, less often a handwritten letter. And nearly every day two or three flyers, addressed to him personally when Chopin had carelessly let himself get stuck in some file, caught in the web of a list. Most tenants blindly discarded these tracts in the large common bin, others gave them merely a glance. Out of habit and principle, all the while worrying the paper between his fingers like fabric, Chopin read them all.

Apart from a postcard and the catalogue of a specialized book dealer in Zurich, the day's ads concerned a singles' club and a plumber, while a third, emanating from a travel agency, proposed an Adriatic cruise under sunny skies, from Otranto to Venice with a stop in Rimini. *Rimini renewed,* said the pamphlet. "Christ!" thought Chopin.

A little girl had just pushed open the building door with great effort, run across the foyer, and bounded into the elevator, her steps replicating the supple echoes of a young monkey in a baobab, but Chopin heard none of this: he was still staring at the flyer. He folded it in four and slipped it into his jacket pocket, stuffed the mail into his other pocket, and, returning to the elevator, Nacera I love you, rode back up to his apartment.

He unfolded the flyer on his desk, his lamp lit even though the sky rushed whole through the panes. He went to the bathroom to fetch alcohol and cotton, then looked in a drawer for an X-Acto blade and two glass slides that he cleaned with the alcohol, with care, sitting at his desk. Then, leaning over the flyer, he enlarged the word *Rimini* with his magnifying glass, heading for the dot over the median *i.*

Calculating the best angle for detaching this dot from its support, Chopin slid the cutting edge of his blade along the typographical sign, which came unglued, unstuck, and tumbled down from Rimini toward one of the glass slides; Chopin caught it under the other slide and fastened the two together with tape. Then he stood up and went to get the enlarger, stored in its box on the floor of the entryway closet at the foot of the vacuum cleaner, between empty suitcases and stacks of journals, among twenty-six unoccupied shoes. Having had nothing to put under its lens for some time, the enlarger was extremely dusty. Chopin wiped it off and settled down to work.

Once the microdot was developed, enlarged, and viewed through a slide projector, its contents consisted of a series of letters that made no immediate sense, organized in groups of four, embellished with little black boxes here and there. Chopin read the arrangement several times, searching his memory for two or three elementary grids; he found the key fairly quickly. The text was not too cruelly coded: he entered it by a double substitution technique, using the Vigenère Tableau. "You haven't lost your touch," said the microdot. "We're glad." It was signed Colonel Seck and followed by a suggested meeting, in one hour at Square Louis XVI.

Letting the square's gate close by itself, Chopin thus headed one hour later toward the expiatory chapel that stood in its center. At the building's threshold, a limping guardian dressed in a traditional blue uniform handed him a brand-new brochure describing this not overly attractive monument, a cube-temple with a small dome introduced by a Doric peristyle. Chopin perused it like anyone else as he walked down the stairs, at the foot of which, standing before the dark marble altar, a midnight blue-clad sexagenarian with very white teeth seemed to be meditating. "It's been a long time," said Colonel Seck.

"Three years," Chopin specified. "We've never met here before, have we?"

"The monument is out-of-the-way," said Colonel Seck. "No one around. It's so depressing, and people aren't *that* desperate. Would you have a bit of time these days?"

"It all depends," said Chopin.

"Perfect," the colonel translated. "I might be in need of your services one of these days. Don't stray too far."

"But I thought," went Chopin hopelessly.

"I know," the colonel admitted, "I know."

They resurfaced toward ground level; the chapel guardian was waiting at the top of the stairs. Ignoring Chopin, he made a beeline for Seck, swaying humble shoulders, his pupil tilting upward beneath his visor. "Colonel," he said, "do you remember Roquette?"

"My word," said Seck, "the name doesn't immediately ring a bell."

"Roquette, Colonel. Blida, the night of the third, the rebels' surprise attack, and then Roquette, Colonel, a ruddy sort. Saxophonist in the 4th Engineering, don't you remember? He's looking for something, he's got problems. He'd like to start over, like me."

"Fine, I'll see what I can do," said Seck. "Tell him to write me a note, just send it there."

He extracted a minuscule card from his jacket, briefly wincing as if he were pulling an extraneous chest hair. The guardian moved a bit closer, his iris confidential. "What should we do, Colonel?" he whispered through his nostrils. "What can we do together for this country?"

"We'll be in touch, Fernandez," Seck murmured, impatiently handing him the calling card. "We'll keep you posted. Be a good fellow, now, and fall out."

Grabbing Chopin by the sleeve and yanking him toward the square's exit, he explained all the cares associated with watching over the retirement of these men who were too old and damaged to keep fighting: "Of course, it's not my job to look after them myself. There's a special department for that, perfectly capable case workers. But things go faster when they come through me and they know it."

He was silent all the way to the gate, which he pulled, holding it open, stopping at the square's threshold to speak again, the way one might tell one's guest the main thing when seeing him out, on the landing while waiting for the elevator:

"You'll get your full instructions in a few days. If there's a problem, I can always be reached by the phone booth on Rue Lafayette, you know, at the corner of Rue Bleue."

For a moment he tilted his forehead toward his long, black, very shiny shoes, imagining himself on his own pedestal; then he snapped his fingers in the void. A green taxi instantly pulled up beside him. He plunged inside and shut the door before giving his destination. The green car and the colonel left the perceptible world via the western length of Boulevard Haussmann; Chopin began walking in the opposite direction. A very pretty redhead crossed the boulevard with a backpack, oh, no, it's a baby, what do you know, then an empty café offered its services on Rue Lavoisier. The proprietor seemed like a caseless judge at his bar. Chopin chose a seat by the large window.

"Coffee," he uttered tersely. "And a glass of water."

These words echoed in the deserted establishment, then silence returned, pierced through at regular intervals by the synthetic voice of a pinball machine that reiterated its presence by emitting the same formula every five minutes. Welcome, Doctor Bong.

Chopin pondered the surface of his coffee, absorbed as if in a movie screen, projecting on it a clip from his first meeting with Colonel Seck—his recruitment, in other words. He had been going through a bit of a Sahara back then, and the colonel's offer seemed not altogether inappropriate, richly hued, gilt-edged, and finely dappled with a hint of blackmail. It would provide a convenient oasis; he accepted. He had immediately been trained in the use of microdots and blank carbon, dead drops, the art of losing tails, and all the rest of that crap. Remember, I'm only doing this for a little while, he'd specified at one point; it's just for a year or two, don't forget. You're absolutely right, the colonel had exclaimed, a year or two, that's exactly what one should tell oneself. Besides, just between you and me, the best of us all said the same thing at first. Welcome, Doctor Bong.

Chopin downed this excellent memory in one gulp, then relaxed in his seat. Patting his pockets, he found the morning's mail, which he opened with the handle of his coffee spoon. The bookseller from Zurich sent him a recension of out-of-print entomological works of which he owned several copies—they would end up knowing everything there is to know about those flies, after which there would be nothing more to say about them. Perhaps they had already reached that point, moreover, which would explain why Chopin had all the time in the world, glued like those flies to the large window. Only the postcard remained, one of its sides depicting a calm ocean. *I'll be waiting for you Wednesday evening at my place,* said the other side. *Suzy.*

Seven

So on WEDNESDAY evening he showed up at her place; it was the first time he'd come after dark. Suzy had nothing to drink but a drop of sorghum liquor, brought back from China by a friend and sticky as old candy. They nonetheless had two or three shots of the stuff, and Thursday morning, before opening the first eyelid, they were already moving against each other, examining and exploring every detail, plains and valleys, ravines and hills, interchanges and one-way paths—all this might have gone on forever, but the alarm clock had just rung.

They spent one more short moment kissing, then Suzy got up. Chopin watched her reach down toward a kind of Japanese robe: her very white back shot through with beauty marks sketched the negative of a summer's night, a constellation on her shoulder with the North Star in the curve of her hip. Then she left the room to go see to Jim, whose twelve-tone intergalactic siren had been bearing witness to his awakening for some time already.

As the bed was growing cold, Chopin got up in turn, dressed while gazing out the courtyard window. The mirror factory hadn't yet opened its doors, but the other one was already vomiting its thin, tireless, immaculate spurt, as if perpetually called upon to announce the election of a new pontiff, an *habemus papam ad libitum*. Two cars were parked at the back of the courtyard; their gleaming hoods reflected the building facades, which reached into the sky.

Behind the closed door the clatter of breakfast cups echoed.

He had just tucked in his shirt when Suzy reentered the room, dressed up to her mirror earrings, her very red lips giving off a quick smile. Indicating to Chopin that coffee was made, she searched in a drawer for her Geneva cuff links, which she fixed to her wrists then quickly showed him, smiling once more: when Suzy was in a hurry the magnetized needles, already jittery, quivered as strongly as if they were approaching the North Pole. She went as she'd come, leaving the door ajar, rushing toward the deep heart of the jungle with her compass and mirror. Chopin adjusted the knot of his tie before leaving the bedroom.

Dressed in an apple-green sweatsuit over whose thigh paraded the yellow words *Carolina Moon*, the young Jim Clair was sitting alone in the kitchen before an amalgam of cereals and a carton of chocolate cookies. He returned Chopin's greeting, pointed to the coffee pot, and dove back into a *Super Giant Uncle Scrooge*. The telephone rang in the main room; they heard Suzy pick up. Chopin drank a little coffee while looking around him: on an armchair, a cat sat absolutely still, as if dead.

Suzy stayed on the phone for quite a while. Her forward-leaning bust was suddenly framed in the doorway, held back by the spiral of the telephone cord, one hand covering the receiver: "Jim, it's eight o'clock," she whispered forcefully, "kindly get ready."

"Yeah, yeah," said Jim.

"I'm coming, Franck," she added.

"Yes," smiled Chopin.

"So," Jim said unexpectedly. "You like my mom?"

Chopin's spoon twirled in the cup under its own steam; he tried to trap it while pondering the question. "Children should be seen and not heard," he limited himself to suggesting.

"The rules have changed," young Jim informed him.

Once Chopin had left for Avenue des Ternes, Suzy brought her son to school, the density of children on the sidewalks increasing as they got closer. Jim said *Hey* to some of them, in a distant tone. A few briefly consulted him in whispers, in one or two words, about some swimming pool or homework business, while throwing circumspect glances Suzy's way; Jim settled matters. His mother, too, greeted the other mothers: the young and beautiful ones with triumphant smiles, but she also had a kind word for the defeated.

She made a large detour via Place Malesherbes up to the Parc Monceau on her way home. While walking, she rummaged in her bag among her keys and papers, her Kleenexes, a datebook containing a photo of Jim at age five, a blue woollen sock from the same Jim at age two used for holding change, a homeopathic vial, two Band-Aids, a hairpin, a stainless steel clip, and a tube of lipstick. From this bag she pulled out a pair of ultra-light headphones with a stem like a spider's leg and clamped them to her ears, then chose one of the cassettes lying at the bottom of the bag, a quintet in C-major that she listened to only as far as the scherzo. Among these tapes there was also a Berlitz Russian course, the voice of her astrologer charting her horoscope for the next two years, *Their Satanic Majesties Request* and *Let It Bleed,* and the soundtracks from three or four films. She picked one of the soundtracks at random, listened to a few lines of repartee ("Cognac? Before dinner? Why not?"), then *andante sostenuto* she returned to the quintet in C.

Once in front of the Parc Monceau, Suzy didn't feel like crossing the gates' ornaments toward the lawns' orderliness. She now headed home. Elderly workers emerging from the mirror factory carried long cheval glasses without looking into them, no longer interested in the reflection of their persons, their labors, and everything that went with them. Below Rue de Rome, the Dieppe local intersected with an express bound for Brest.

She straightened house a bit—the kitchen, then the bedrooms, and by capillarity everywhere else—vaguely checking to see if Chopin might have forgotten some object, or even left one there on purpose; but no, nothing. At around eleven, she sat at the table in her bedroom and began work, which these days consisted of writing a catalogue of accessories for wealthy ladies—easy and well-remunerated work, which the typewriter wrote almost by itself, each *ding* at the end of a line announcing the birth of a plump little banknote. Short and close together, two rings at the door straddled the dings of the typewriter bell. Having lowered the radio's variety shows, Suzy got up to answer them.

The visitor was a well-built young man sporting a crew cut, a signet ring on each pinky, a chain around his neck. Drenched in very fragrant aftershave, he smiled, exuding health as if he'd just stepped from the shower, eye half-closed on a soap bubble that had gotten in. "Come in, Frédéric," Suzy smiled with moderation; then she turned back toward the main room, letting her visitor close the door himself. "Caramba!" he silently exclaimed as he followed her, "that's got to be the best pair of legs in the greater Paris area." Crossing these legs after having sat, Suzy motioned toward a chair and the visitor took a seat, averting his gaze.

"I think I might have something," said this young Frédéric. "I think I told you, I have a friend who can get in there, I mean, who maybe could explain the thing to you himself, in a few days."

"When?" Suzy wanted to know.

Eight

O~N ANOTHER MORNING~ after the morning after, Chopin sat at home, not too far from the window as always, idle as so often early in the morning, alone as usual.

Alone: Carole and Marianne had lived there by turns, only to leave in dismay at the end of several days or weeks, returning later then leaving again, in regular succession. Chopin never did anything to make them go or stay, leaving his door open in both directions. Carole took fashion photographs and Marianne hosted films on television, so that even when they disappeared from his life Chopin sometimes had indirect news of them. They had nothing in common, although once, three days apart, each had asked him to go in with her (thanks to special fee reductions offered by their respective job benefits) in joining a health club.

Chopin trimmed his nails while watching the weather fade to grey through the panes. Then he went to fetch a banana in the kitchen, gradually after each bite stripping back the four or five lashes of skin that covered his closed fist like faded petals; carefully detaching the friable, cardboard-flavored filaments that ran along its surface in meridians—in short, peeling his banana as the anthropoid will eternally peel its own. He dropped one of the filaments into the fly cage.

Colonel Seck's fond greetings presented themselves at eleven o'clock, at the opening of the mailboxes. This time it was not

Rimini but Mississippi that harbored a new microdot, setting a meeting with Chopin at number 22 of a backstreet hidden in the sixteenth arrondissement. To get there, he had to apply the classic procedure for discouraging tails, and it was once more and forever the same rigmarole: you hop from one taxi into the metro entrance, then from another taxi into another metro, and you jump into the train at the last instant, and you jump off the train just before the doors close, and you cross and recross the building with double exits, then another building, and you hop yet another taxi that drops you fifty yards from the hidden backstreet, which you reach in a sweat, out of breath and certain that this whole business is utterly pointless. And you see that number 22, built around 1960, is an apartment house with smoked-glass balconies such as one finds not so much in Paris as in the provinces, especially in seaside towns, where retirees enjoy direct access to the grounds.

The colonel welcomed Chopin into an empty apartment. The huge foyer was bare, except for a clothes tree on which the only thing hanging was a bent, empty can of white paint, by its handle. Chopin followed his case officer into a hallway, at whose midpoint the muffled sounds of construction seeped through a sealed doorway. On the hallway walls, delineating the placement of vanished images, the former inhabitants' thumbtacks were still hanging, and the fresh boxes pushed against the baseboard must have belonged to the next batch. There remained only the promotional calendar of a sushi bar on Rue Washington, its use discontinued as of the previous August, showing two white rabbits on a field of snow and giving the address (Nishishinjuku Shinjuku-Ku) of another sushi bar in Tokyo.

Seck opened the door to a living room in which two desk chairs faced each other, a polished brown-leather briefcase resting at the feet of one of them. On a wall, among the useless thumbtacks still planted there, hung a solitary frame containing green-and-white shapes. The colonel offered Chopin one of the desk chairs while moving toward the French doors that led to a balcony: the ghosts of plants hugged the earth at the bottom of faded window boxes, in a cocoon of dehydrated humus. The colonel's forehead pressed against the window; his eyes pondered the nonexistent traffic in the backstreet. A dull and dusty light fell on him.

"There are days when I miss the sun," he said. "The tropical sun, and all that. Sex and the tropics. I get awfully bored sometimes, you can't imagine."

He spread his arms in a desolate way, then returned to sit in silence. Chopin recalled that in these situations, it was not his place to speak first.

"So," the colonel finally said, "I've got a small observation problem, if you see what I mean. Right now I don't have anyone on hand to take care of it, so I thought of you. Let me explain."

So: a summit of economic leaders, gathering various Eastern and Western delegations, had just closed in Vienna. One of the experts had not immediately returned to his country of origin, allowing himself a few days' rest in the Paris area. The colonel paused and leaned toward the briefcase, from which he pulled two books. He handed one to Chopin, a rather thin bound volume, printed on yellowish paper that gave off a vigorous industrial odor, and covered with a stagnant green jacket bearing the title of the work and the name of its author: *Perspectives on the Arkhangelsk Colloquium* by Vital Veber. A portrait of the latter was reproduced on the jacket flap: from the center of a dark rectangle emerged a slightly hazy face, no doubt an enlarged detail from a group photograph. His features were no more visible than those of a condemned man through the wicket of an obscure jail, or those of a prompter in his hole.

"An important fellow," grumbled Colonel Seck. "Former first secretary of the district, general secretary in charge of the economic plan, spokesman for the surface committee, you know the type."

As the construction noise had suddenly increased, he stood up, looking miffed. "I'll be right back," he predicted. "You can glance at that one, too, while waiting." Chopin picked up the other volume, similar in every respect to the first except for the title (*The Lessons of the Anchorage Conference*), the washed-out beige nuance of the jacket, and two minuscule retouches to the author photo. He began leafing through the two works while listening in on the sounds of voices that reached him from the hallway, no doubt originating in the kitchen: muffled and annoyed, Colonel Seck's seemed to run up against two other voices, female, and full of reason, good sense, and mocking aplomb. A fat silence concluded the exchange, then the colonel returned, his face taut.

"These renovations will never be over," he groused. "I want one lousy thing and you'd think I was asking for the moon. That boiler is new, it's practically new, what do they have to go change everything for?" He worked himself up into a lather while Chopin continued studying the portrait of Vital Veber: no doubt a once-sharp universitarian countenance, gradually thickened by dignities, creased by the cares proper to all general secretaries.

"So," the colonel resumed. "That's the guy. What do you think?"

"Not much," answered Chopin. "But I don't suppose I have a whole lot of choice."

"That's right, complain," went the colonel. "Look, I'm not asking you for much. What'll it take you, not even half your time, barely a quarter, and even then? Not even."

"Okay," said Chopin, "all right."

"It would really help us out," the other amplified gently, "it would really be great. And besides, it's nothing complicated, which is also great. Veber is going to spend a week in a hotel, nice place, not far from Paris. It's a gorgeous spot, in a park by a lake, quite pleasant. All you have to do is spend a week there, too, at the same time he does."

Chopin didn't answer, laboring in vain to identify the contents of the frame hung near the French doors at the other end of the living room: five white rectangles on a billiard-green background.

"Remember, I don't want to force you into anything," his case officer continued, "but there it is. As I said, I thought of you. I think of you often, Chopin. I like you, whatever you might imagine. Do you find that amusing?"

"Not at all," said Chopin. "I don't find it amusing at all."

"Anyway, there we are," the colonel darkened. "You'll have to see what this guy's up to, who he meets, that sort of thing. And maybe see if someone else isn't trying to see along with us, eh?"

"Absolutely," said Chopin. "A bit like with Abitbol."

The memory of Abitbol cheered the military man.

"Exactly," he hammered out with satisfaction. "Just like with Abitbol. In theory, Veber's traveling with his assistant, his secretary, I'm not sure which. What else can I tell you?"

All at once, four terrifying sledgehammer blows rang out in the hallway, making the windows tremble and the colonel jump. "What the hell are they up to?" he murmured.

"I was wondering what the hell they're up to," he explained

for Chopin's benefit. "They gave me an estimate. I was perfectly happy with the estimate. Now I don't get it, it seems to have no relation to anything anymore."

"Is this *your* apartment?"

"Come see," said the colonel, standing. "It wasn't my salary that did this. Come take a look: this is how I paid for it."

He pulled Chopin toward the green-and-white frame. On a baize background, under non-reflecting glass, five playing cards forming a quint flush were arranged in a fan—seven and eight, nine and ten of hearts gracefully spread out on either side of the jack, like sirens around Esther Williams.

"August 1985, Beaulieu-sur-Mer," specified the colonel. "A million three. It happened to me. I was able to buy this thing. It's not very big, but what can you do. Anyway, I'm in the process of selling it. Then something else, a bit of land out where I come from. Where were we?"

"Veber," Chopin reminded him. "The hotel."

"Right. The hotel. It would be good if you could use your system again at the hotel. You know?"

"System?" said Chopin.

"You know, your flies. Don't you remember?"

"You're joking," Chopin said. "It's completely outdated. Those techniques date back to General Walters's time. These days they do it much better."

Disappointed, the colonel hazarded that if he remembered correctly, the fly technique had nonetheless yielded excellent results, for example with that same Abitbol. But Chopin highlighted the fact that this technique had strict limitations: that a fly lasted only a short while; that the lifespan of a fly was a mere blink.

"Let's try it all the same," the colonel insisted. "Let's try it."

As a seismic grumbling of machine tools had now risen in the kitchen, he couldn't help inspecting the labors en route to seeing Chopin out; the latter glanced over his shoulder. The two contractors were short and stout, their thick cheeks tending to droop, their greasy, plaster-flecked hair hanging limp. On top of which, they did not seem particularly accommodating, one unraveling copper wire between her butcher-like red fingers, the other drilling a wall with two spare bits between her teeth. Nonetheless, just like two socialist-realist laborers they were smiling; their entire bodies beamed victoriously beneath blue overalls that were stuffed like sausages.

"And what the hell's this thing, now?" the colonel exploded. "What's this hole for? It seems to me this hole wasn't in the estimate. Why do we need this hole?"

"Automatic circuit breaker for the boiler," drill bits explained. "For safety. It wouldn't hurt to have the conduit cleaned out once in a while, eh?"

"But there was none of that before," the officer moaned, "and it worked just fine. And besides, there's the wire. That circuit breaker's going to need a wire, and you'll see it. It's going to look like crap."

"We'll conceal it for you," the other jovially assured him. "Hey, don't worry, it'll be concealed."

The colonel shrugged one shoulder and quickly moved away from the laborers, murmuring *Goddamn bitches* as soon as he was out of earshot. In the foyer, in a distracted voice, he mentioned that they'd meet later for the final instructions, somewhere else. Here it was really too complicated at the moment. Well, thanks for coming in any case. Thank you.

Nine

THAT SAME DAY, even as Chopin was disrobing his bananas, young Frédéric was once again heading for Rue de Rome. Shaved even closer than two days ago, the prow of his aftershave even more cutting, Frédéric sliced efficiently through the air. After he'd rung twice, Suzy came to open the door in bare feet, wrapped in a large red terry-cloth bathrobe, one hand on the door handle, the other holding a tan square of towel to her hair.

She let the young man in, then took shelter in the bathroom, absentmindedly cursing him. She slipped on a large, sand-colored sweater, a pair of black shorts, and grey-pink suede thigh-boots, and hung green loops of wide diameter from her ears. When she returned to the kitchen all was silence, Jim having cut himself off from the world and its wafts of aftershave behind a *Pif Super Comic*. After several fruitless attempts at contact, Frédéric had retreated toward the mute television: with maps bearing witness, an auburn meteorologist was moving her lips.

"It's urgent," the young man said as soon as Suzy reappeared.

"Later," she went softly, with a discreet gesture, a sidelong glance toward Jim, "in a minute."

Suzy poured some corn flakes into the child's bowl, as the latter suddenly hopped off his chair, having spotted the opening credits of a television game show identified as funny. "No, Jim," she protested, "we don't have time."

"It's really short, it's really really short," Jim assured her, abruptly and exaggeratedly turning up the sound, AND WHAT DO YOUR PARENTS DO, FABIENNE? WELL, UM, MY DAD IS A FOREMAN AND MY MOM'S A HOUSEWIFE. WONDERFUL, FABIENNE, THAT'S JUST GREAT AND HERE'S OUR FIRST QUESTION, until Suzy had to shout, "No, no, turn it down—would you like an apple, Frédéric? They're good for you."

He was about to accept but she was already looking elsewhere, stacking cups on a tray. "It's just about time," she said. "Get dressed, go on, quick."

"Can I give you a hand?" Frédéric proposed in the din.

"I said turn off that TV," Suzy ordered firmly. OH, FABIENNE, I'M SO SORRY.

"So," she said to Frédéric half an hour later, "it wasn't so urgent after all."

They were coming back from bringing Jim to school, walking less quickly than in the other direction. After the widespread rush toward offices, factories, and schools, the streets were calmer. Everything caught its breath before the next starter shot; the street sweepers dusted the asphalt casually, sparingly.

"It's just that I'm supposed to see my friend," said Frédéric. "The guy I told you about Thursday, I'm supposed to see him in a little while. I wanted to let you know. I mean, I do have to keep you posted."

"I don't really believe in it anymore," she said in a distracted voice. "I just don't know."

"You could act a bit more interested," Frédéric timidly flared up. "This *is* your husband we're talking about, after all."

She smiled a blank smile into the monotonous emptiness.

"And me doing this for you," he added a bit more shrilly, "me doing this just because it's for you. Do you know a lot of guys who'd spend their time looking for the love of their life's husband?"

They had arrived in front of her building and Frédéric lowered his head with a pouty expression. Suzy smiled more brightly at him, amused in three dimensions. "You're sweet," she said, briefly touching her lips to one of the young man's cheeks. One of the green loops hanging from her ears rang like a gong against Frédéric's nose, like thunder in a clear sky, and the next instant she was no longer there, vaporized under the effect of that kiss.

Ten

THE PARC PALACE DU LAC is situated in the middle of a wooded stretch of land bordering an ample expanse of freshwater, over which a flat boat sometimes carries the hotel guests. This establishment, with its twenty rooms and suites, places at its guests' disposal a restaurant, two bars, three conference rooms, and laundry and dry cleaning services. The salaries of a very qualified staff of chefs, porters, switchboard operators, chambermaids, and assorted bellboys justifies the cost of a single night. Standing outside the normal hotel circuits, the Parc Palace is a quiet, secluded building, often frequented by clients who are incognito, and who in any case are too rich and powerful to be known to the general public. Its name does not appear in any guidebook.

The general secretary Vital Veber, for his part, is situated in an automatic-drive Peugeot, which has just turned into the private alleyway leading to the Parc Palace du Lac. This man, with his sixty years of experience, is traveling with his cryptanalyst, two briefcases full of files, three suitcases of clothes, and a shortwave transmitter. The company of a committee of experts, financiers, urban planners, economists, jurists, and assorted researchers occupies each of his days and more than one of his nights. Always standing apart from official functions, Vital Veber is a quiet, reserved man, pleasant to his colleagues, who in any case are too scrupulous and devoted to take offense. His name does not figure in *Who's Who*.

Away from the apparatchiks, away from the paparazzi, the general secretary was getting ready to enjoy several days of well-deserved rest. His airplane, a Fairchild 227 twin-engined prop-jet, had landed early that morning at Orly Airport. The cryptanalyst had claimed the car at the rental desk and they had been off, Veber himself behind the wheel of the Peugeot. He moved it along slowly, having lost the habit of driving and never acquired that of automatic transmissions. Four hundred yards behind the Peugeot, a Renault with similar cubic capacity rolled at the same speed, containing two young security persons named Perla Pommeck and Rodion Rathenau, short blond hair and alert grey eyes, supple suit and ensemble and two hours of physical conditioning every day. It was a cool outer-suburban morning. The air was light as a salad, dry and crisp as white wine; it clearly delineated the building facades and gently rested on the rooftops.

For a moment the Peugeot was stopped by a railroad crossing gate. With the nose of its hood resting against the bicolored arm, under the cross of blinking red lights, its two occupants watched the wagons parade by, meeting the furtive glances of the passengers under the triple horn of the rail car: two trebles separated by a bass one octave lower.

Vital Veber pushed a button to lower his window and let the sound into the car, distorted by the train's movement. Then he jutted his elbow outside, pondering two dogs alone in the world who sniffed each other artlessly on their segment of curb, circled each other feverishly, and naturally failed to climb onto one another at the same time. Veber had difficulty turning away from this spectacle, to which he abstained from drawing the attention of the cryptanalyst, who was himself absorbed in a road map spread over his knees like a plaid blanket. Instead, he noted that things didn't seem to have changed much here since 1955. "That's true," said the cryptanalyst. "They haven't really done much to the area."

The tail of the train having fled, the barriers having opened the road, the Peugeot covered another mile and a half before veering into the hotel entrance. No plaque signaled the existence of the Parc Palace du Lac, which was invisible from the highway. There was merely a complicated fence made of steel cuttings, framed by two impersonal marble columns, grave and tidy like majordomos, one of them decorated with an intercom button. The cryptanalyst stepped out of the car to press it.

"Veber," he said into it. "We've reserved number nine."

The fence, in turn, freed access to the narrow path that wound beneath beech and ash, among cubes of bush and squares of lawn. In all this greenery, one occasionally began to see a man on foot carrying a golf club or racket; one passed by tennis courts, stables in the distance, then the croquet lawn, the giant chess board. Soon one finally made out the large, dusty-rose body of the Parc Palace, huddled onto itself and slightly hunched, reassuring like a kindly millionnaire. "That's fine," said Veber. "We'll be fine here. Don't you think this is fine?" The cryptanalyst nodded, pursing his lips in a sign of measured acquiescence.

"That northeast file," Veber resumed after a silence. "Do you think we can get that squared away quickly?"

"The analysis is nothing," the other answered. "No more than a day or two. What's going to take time is seeing if it matches Ratine's report."

"And there's also the surface committee," the secretary general pointed out. "There's that, too. And all the bureau's amendments."

"Let's leave that for the end," the cryptanalyst suggested. "It would be better to examine the committee's amendments as a last step. Don't forget that first we have to index everything according to the new Boyadjian-Goldfarb standards. These days, that's their only method of induction."

"Good Lord," Veber started, "I'd completely forgotten about Boyadjian-Goldfarb. Do *you* know the new standards?"

"Goldfarb showed me the draft," the cryptanalyst said calmly. "I should be able to reconstruct the key, more or less."

"Perfect," Veber concluded while pulling the hand brake.

They got out of the Peugeot. Already the bellboys were swiftly emptying the trunk, then the parking valet made the car vanish toward the garages behind a line of elms. Vital Veber preceded his cryptanalyst by one step onto the stairway, at the bottom of which Perla Pommeck and Rodion Rathenau had discreetly stationed themselves, faces impassive and glances circular.

Starting at the hotel entrance, this stairway slid in a gentle decline, like a dying wave absorbed by the gravel, flanked by banisters at support height that flared out as of the first steps to encircle at their summit a long terrace furnished with white armchairs and white pedestal tables beneath blue parasols. At the heart of the terrace—the navel of the Parc Palace—protected by a fan-shaped glass awning, four tall, ogival, vitreous doors advanced toward the world in a concave arc, opening onto the hotel foyer. And beneath the glass roof, arched in iron-grey evening wear between two rows of red bellboys, the manager of the Parc Palace du Lac awaited the new arrivals.

Each suite was composed of a living room, a bedroom, a dressing room that was a little too large for a dressing room, and a bathroom for extended families. An unobstructed view of the terrace, gravel paths, and lawns spread before them, as previously arranged from the secretary general's apartment. In the afternoon he went to visit his cryptanalyst, the windows of whose room, on the other hand, were masked by nearby trees. Through the filter of their leaves one could barely make out the expanse of the lake beyond the golf course. The walls of his dressing room were solid; the only light came from a chandelier. "We might as well work here," suggested Veber, "if that's all right with you. With another lamp or two, it will do just fine. In any case, we won't begin until tomorrow. See you this evening."

The only problem at dinner was that the names of the dishes were a bit abstract. The general secretary hesitated between the Affect of squint pheasant on a chiffon of rampion and the Saint-Evremond tulle of perch in sherry. He questioned the cryptanalyst, then the maitre d', but as their hypotheses could not dispel his fears he decided that first evening to limit himself to the shortest name, something entitled Beef brouillon Bobigny.

"You choose the wine. Anyway, never fear, we won't spend all our time working. First we'll take care of the northeast, that's the only pressing case, and then did you see they have a golf course here? Do you play?"

"Not very often," admitted the cryptanalyst.

"Five under par myself," Veber said with pleasure. "If you like, you could come with me for three or four holes. You won't want to stray too far from the hotel, I suppose—neither do I. Just a couple of errands to run in Paris during the week, perhaps, and even then. Otherwise, I'm not moving. It's so quiet here."

Pulling from his pocket a flyer found in his room, which detailed the services offered by the Parc Palace du Lac, he recited the characteristics of the giant chess board spotted that morning on arrival: each square was the size of four standard chess boards and every piece—life-sized kings and queens, pawns in preadolescent format—were mounted on ball bearings; for next season they promised fully jointed horses for the knights. "That's nothing new," Veber noted, yawning. "They've got more or less the same at Baden-Baden."

Eleven

AT THE HOUR when general secretaries go to bed, snug and warm in their vacation resort, Chopin discovered the new prospectus as he returned home, Nacera I love you still.

After a while, Chopin stopped feeling much enjoyment in seeking out the microdot in the flyer text, detaching it, developing it, enlarging it, then decoding it; even espionage can get stale, after a while. It's just that the trade has its monotonies and its chores: for example, one still has four hours to kill before answering the colonel's latest summons, far out in the suburbs.

While waiting in front of the television, Chopin spent a moment watching programs parade by while he dined on a chicken sandwich: a dark-haired singer, a light-haired singer, Rwandan animals, some high-diving, and two fiction series. *I have a margin of decision independent of any authority,* warned the star android of one of the series. *Wait!* a prognathous secondary character panicked in the other. *Orders to kill the monster have been rescinded!* Chopin returned to the singer, who was dressed in a skimpy black ensemble with black mitts; behind her, the band, composed of three lucid and relaxed young individuals, grinned the full width of their eighty-eight keys.

Then he took a very long bath while other singers succeeded one another on the radio. Immobile in the hollow of his tub, only his corseless head protruded from the liquid, among filaments of foam and bubbles, and hairs fallen out during shampooing that floated, scarcely visible, just below the surface. Chopin pondered his body refracted in the wavering block. He took stock of its various stigmata, barbarous scars with delicate stitching: the effects of surgery, accidents, punches. He located and dated each one, from the gash on his knee (Baccarat, 1957) to the stiffness in one metacarpal (Canton, 1980), and then the bruises—but you can't always tell where those fleeting bruises come from. All the while he periodically added some hot water and lent an ear to the different songstresses on the radio, the opaque and the vehement, the infantile and the jaded. When each had sung her song, when none remained, Chopin emerged from his bath.

Seated on the arm of a chair at around one in the morning, armed with his nail scissors, he unstitched the labels of his clothing, as he had been trained to do back in the good old days. At around two o'clock, dressed again, he skimmed through the contents of a recently received flyer, then two or three digests, as well as the news-in-brief column relating the activities of learned societies; in the bibliography of a longitudinal study concerning nine generations of *Dipter antiphrisson,* they cited one of the first articles of his career, devoted to moth flies.*

At around three o'clock, when Chopin exited Paris via Porte d'Orléans, it was raining lightly. His car settled into the left-hand lane of the highway, passing a row of empty semitrailers, then veered onto an exit ramp flanked by road signs that announced the national food market. After that it skirted the fenced avenue

---

* Chopin, F., "Experimental Conditions of Autonomous Flight Performance in Psychodidae (*Psychoda alternata*)," *Annals of Parasitology,* xx:6, pp. 467–73.

circling said market, larded with video cameras whose job it was to inform the central tower about the vehicular traffic. In the line at the entrance tollbooth, the Karmann Ghia sat like a dwarf among the double-undercarriages of truck tires; under other batteries of cameras, billboards in the Arabic and Portuguese tongues reiterated the prohibition against retail transactions within the confines of the national food market. After the tolls, having rounded the cut-flower pavilion, Chopin wound past massive constructions containing everything that can be eaten in Eastern Europe.

A somber six-lane boulevard, scanned by glazed streetlamps, encircled a vast mercantile zone criss-crossed with alleys and streets at ninety-degree angles. Approaching the center, Chopin began seeing furtive preview sketches between the edifices: men dressed in bloody white handing each other sides of beef, or fifteen fish dead in vain biting the dust at the entrance to the seafood pavilion, or a lone driver charming a hundred-yard snake of carts.

The slaughterhouse pavilion, the site of his rendezvous with Colonel Seck, was built separate from the others, discreetly relegated to the other side of the circular boulevard. As tall as your basic basilica and wide as an Australian football field, the pavilion was a large mass enclosed at both ends by thick sheets of soft, translucent plastic that one pushed aside to enter: inside they treated whatever remained after the meat had been removed and the skeleton recycled, whatever could be recovered between skin and bone; there they dealt in cartilage and viscera; there a brain trust of tripe experts swayed hearts and kidneys.

Near the entrance opposite the boulevard, toward the skull-crushing stalls, a row of high metal bins overflowed with yellow and white bones beneath the assorted pallors of the streetlamps.

There Chopin spotted, parked in the shadows on the corner of Rue du Jour, the colonel's midnight blue Opel; its windshield reflected the line of bins in cinemascope.

Chopin pulled up alongside the Opel, shut off his engine, and waited. It was still drizzling. Three minutes passed, as did three forklifts bearing various meat by-products on pallets; then a silhouette came by to dump a load of skulls into one of the bins. After it had vanished, there was no more movement until Chopin saw the blue car door open. He then opened his own door in silence and the rain scarcely touched him, his feet barely grazed the sticky ground; in one leap he found himself in the fat Opel's front seat.

The aroma inside the cockpit was a perfect blend of island rum, island woods, and Havana cigar stub, of Aramis and arabica. Some English-language easy listening droned softly on the whispered froth of conditioned air.

"I'm very fond of this place," said Colonel Seck. "It's lively all night long, it's professional. It's good. Have something, help yourself. Cigar?"

Thrusting his hand under the car radio, he opened an oblong rosewood drawer containing a flask, a nickel-plated thermos, three small bottles, and four tumblers nestled in their felt gangue.

"Just some coffee," said Chopin, "thanks."

"Veber arrived this morning," the colonel announced. "The hotel isn't too far from here—you'll see."

There followed various details concerning the schedules and means of transport employed by the general secretary. "I don't know his room number," the case officer apologized, "but I've got someone on site, he can tell you. Two other people arrived at the same time he did, of course, that was to be expected. A guy and a girl—both very athletic, if you get my drift."

The English-language easy listening had just ended, and the colonel looked for more by pushing the frequency selector buttons, passing through all kinds of music that didn't suit him, as well as low voices launched into the ether, disk jockeys straddling the void, whose tense inflections betrayed their anxiety at talking alone without reaching anyone at all.

"So who's your on-site?" Chopin wanted to know.

"Mouezy-Eon," said the colonel. "Remember him? He'll be around in case you need a hand—although I can't promise much there, eh? He's just about had it, Mouezy-Eon. He's slowing down."

Seck continued searching for the right music as he talked; Chopin poured a few drops of rum into the dregs of his coffee and looked straight ahead. Outside the light precipitation continued. Droplets of rain hunched on the glass, sparse and immobile. They had to band together, get unionized in one fat drop before they could hurtle gaily down the windshield, on whose verso, inside the car, droplets of fog clustered toward the same end. It sometimes happened that two drops of different nature rolled down at the same time, united on opposite sides of the windshield, appearing to slice it down the middle. Interesting, all right.

"Goddamn radio," the colonel concluded, burrowing in the glove compartment. "So, anyway, you get the picture. What *I* want to know is what the hell Veber's up to. You'll make out fine."

"My powers are limited," Chopin reminded him.

Seck had just found a cassette, which he shoved into the player. "I know," he said, "but don't you think with your flies...?"

"I told you," Chopin reminded him. "It's always the same problem. They die too fast when they're wired. They'd need to last longer."

"Couldn't we fortify them?" the colonel ventured, aiming the butt of his cigar at Chopin. "Give them something?"

Ignoring the suggestion, Chopin said that the best thing would be to use the fattest ones, of course. "They hold out the longest. But the fatter they are, the more noticeable, that's the problem with those bugs. The minute you see a fly, you want to swat it." The cassette had begun to play, unspooling a potpourri of works by Engelbert Humperdinck and Roger Wittaker—pure heaven to Colonel Seck's way of thinking. His foot tapped gently on the brake pedal.

"But even so," Chopin continued, "I can't believe you haven't got anything more sophisticated. With all the things they can do these days."

"We've got," said the colonel, "we've got. But I was caught a bit short. Otherwise I could have whatever I wanted, believe you me. All the directional mikes, long-distance systems, suitcases that can do this and that, sure we've got. It's just that we're completely overworked these days; everything's been taken already."

Behind them, the truck traffic was intensifying. The comings and goings of buyers and sellers, retailers and wholesalers, turned the pavilions into anthills; and in front of them there had been a perceptible increase in the back-and-forth of carcasses. The colonel glanced at his Patek-Philippe and immolated his cigar stub in the ashtray.

"Ten to four, time to go. The tide's coming in any minute, this place'll be crawling in no time. Better to be discreet. Can you start tomorrow?"

There were more heavy trucks on the highway home, too, in an almost uninterrupted line, forming a kind of wildcat military convoy, a mercenary parade with mismatched tarpaulins heading toward the spoils of some food war; but then in Paris it was almost deserted. And all down the petrified avenues, the coupe's motor echoed plaintively against the stone facades, the way a man moans in solitary between four bare walls.

Twelve

I'T'S NOT THAT Suzy was crazy when she was little, of course; she just liked to baptize her body parts: back then, her stomach was called Simon, her liver Judas, her lungs Peter and John. Her heart changed identity at will, having first, at age fourteen, taken that of a certain Robert, the first ever to kiss her. Suzy had been wild about Robert; he wasn't much of a talker, but he was surely the cutest boy in the housing development. For weeks before he managed to kiss her for real, they had held hands for hours at a stretch, sitting side-by-side against the wall near the garages, without speaking, watching the others laugh loudly and rev up their ether-inflated motorbikes; afterward they walked each other home indefinitely throughout the projects, from the foot of one high-rise to the other. After Robert, the succession of names given Suzy's heart was no longer quite so clear. She remembered the ones belonging to the brother of her English pen pal, then to the son of a police-man, and a fair number of mainly dark-haired boys, including a swimming instructor who was rather soft but very, very, very funny. Gérard.

After age twenty, far from Blois, several longer episodes had notably introduced two painters, Charles Esterellas, then Eliseo Schwartz—artists whose portraits of Suzy, later on, in the course of various moves, Oswald would never know where to hang. The one by Esterellas, set against a blast furnace, soon found its niche in the entryway; but things got a bit more complicated with the one by Schwartz, a nude under the shower that Oswald refused to display in the living room, no more than in the bedroom, or, naturally, in the bathroom. Suzy as observed by her ex-lovers, in plain sight of everyone and before Oswald's eyes, thus posed some inconvenience to the Clair couple, even though they had agreed not to throw the paintings out. The showering nude there-fore hung around for a while, relegated to an odd corner, before settling at the back of a closet, where the blast furnace joined it several months later.

Moving into Rue de Rome, Suzy had stashed both paintings in back of the new closet without even unwrapping them, and in the six months following Oswald's disappearance she had hung noth-ing at all on the walls. Then very gradually appeared a postcard or drawing of Jim's leaning on some books or on the mantlepiece, the two reproductions on the walls of her room, and the photo of the maharajas tacked above the desk.

At around ten o'clock she had sat at this desk: two metal sawhorses supporting a large, thick glass pane that held equally transparent objects—the clear brick of the ashtray, the mineral water in its plastic liter bottle—as well as other, more opaque ones: the white paper, the black typewriter, and the red transistor radio through which, at that moment, Gerry Mulligan was blowing fresh air. Suzy wrote quickly, without revising. Through the closed win-dows, the city noise reached her like the damper of a monstrous, repetitive piano, the musician's left hand providing the low rum-blings of traffic in continuous chords, while his right improvised motifs that were swift and jangling, sharp and precise, furnished by bumper crunch and horn blast in Rue de Rome or by breaking glass in the mirror factory. And over it all, the telephone's ring.

"It's me again," said Frédéric. "Can I come by? I'm with a friend, not far from your place. We won't be long."

In the time it would take to open and close the window, they were already there. Frédéric's friend was a very thin, very shy, very tall young man, with a sorrel head of hair styled in a complex brush, DA on his nape and three locks arranged like thrust faults down his forehead. Hairdos must have constituted a separate item in his budget.

"This is Lucien," said Frédéric. "It's an incredible stroke of luck. Tell her, Lucien."

"It's about your husband," the young man blushed.

Without looking Suzy in the eye, he began to speak: his high, slightly raucous voice seemed to emit from rusty glottal stops, and his story swarmed with difficult pauses, commas and semicolons, during which he swallowed a bit of saliva and grimaced, with a painful creaking of the siphon and long round-trips of the Adam's apple. At the end of his story, he sniffed against the pulp of his thumb, a discreet full stop, before silently pondering one of his feet. Suzy watched him curiously.

"But, tell me," she asked gently, "how can you possibly know all that?" Lucien gave her a terrified look, twisted his lips, and turned toward Frédéric.

"He can't tell you," Frédéric assured her paternally. "Confidential matters that he came upon by chance, through his job. If they found out he was telling you this, he could lose it. It's bad enough with the hair. But we won't keep you any longer."

She rose from her seat an instant after they did, briefly glancing around as if she were about to leave a train, making sure she hadn't forgotten anything. The two young men had already left the room and were waiting for her at the end of the hallway; after another slight delay she joined them and opened the door, behind which Chopin stood, finger raised, about to ring. Suzy closed her eyes. "Is something wrong?" said Chopin.

He stood aside, letting by the two young men, who greeted him, politely took their leave, and went off speaking in hushed tones. Suzy saw Lucien glance back at her just before reaching the elevator. Then she didn't seem very attentive when Chopin announced that he had to go out of town for a few days, a week at most, a chore: professionally, he felt obliged to attend a seminar in Marseilles devoted to various parasites, bedbugs, clothes moths, body lice. He tried joking about the aberrant sexuality of the bedbug, who reaches genital satisfaction while perforating her partner during the act, but he didn't seem very sure of himself, either. "Is anything the matter?"

They were silent, standing in the middle of the living room. Chopin hugged Suzy to him, his eyes in her hair, not quite daring to ask what was going on, who those young men were that he'd just met. Her eyes were open, staring over Chopin's shoulder at an everyday, translucent object, white, invisible to common mortals. Still, almost immediately they found themselves in the bedroom, quickly stripping off their clothes as on a beach when someone calls you from the rushing water and you run; the sheets rolled in waves and you dive in, float and swim for a very long time, butterfly and breast stroke; then exhausted you return and fall on the sand amid the knots of terry-cloth towels; silent and drenched you lie still, full of sand and salt and then sweat, you burn, eyelids closed under the shining sun, the blanket of sky.

Thirteen

Tuesday morning, suitcase and trunk in hand, Franck Chopin appeared in the lobby of the Parc Palace du Lac. While the receptionist verified his reservation on the register, Chopin mentally photographed the room keys hanging on the board to form their composite portrait.

Reserved by the colonel's secretariat under the name Bernard Blanchard, the room allotted to Chopin combined elements of traditional French hostelry (shining parquet floor, antique furniture, heavy quilt) with international ultramodern comfort (pulsating shower with stream modulator, remote-controlled blinds and curtains, soft porn cable channel). The wallpaper represented a discreetly tricolored flower motif, repeated on the fabric of the armchairs and the bedspread.

Deflating the eiderdown, Chopin tossed his suitcase on the bed, opened it, and took out his toiletry kit: from between the teeth of his comb he removed a hair, which he pressed to the closet door after having placed his trunk within. Then he stood for a moment in front of the window, from which one could easily see the surface of the lake, a mirror spangled with light motorboats, before going back down to the ground floor. By a process of mental association, Chopin briefly checked his temples in the elevator mirror—a dispatch from the fallen hair front.

Not more than a dozen guests were to be found on the terrace at that hour, on white armchairs loaded with vibrant cushions. Slouching in their midst rested two or three nabobs whose ultraviolet-tanned faces connoted ease and usury, accompanied by mammillary secretaries and vaporous wives. To one side, near the balustrades, a beautiful woman with a lost look, very nervous and very well dressed, cringed while an older, plainer woman consoled her. Nearer the steps was another illegitimate couple with a particularly clinging setter, eternally interposed like a guilty conscience: to touch and kiss, they constantly had to avoid this dog, push away this dog, forge a path of non-dog. Lowering their arms, the lovers finally stood to head off onto the grounds, joined by the indefatigable animal who sprang between them, cavorting among the poplars. Left standing near the hotel doors, under the glass fan, Chopin followed them with his eyes.

Below the terrace, posed on his folding chair, a watercolorist of mature years pocked with little stabs of his brush a raisin-colored surface attached to a tripod. As one of the setter's lurches just missed knocking over the easel, the exasperated lover began quietly threatening the beast—who kept following them, who was ruining their entire stay—with the pound. Chopin moved away from the entrance to the Parc Palace, crossed the terrace, and headed downstairs in the same direction.

Seen from up close, the watercolorist did not seem much older than the lolling nabobs, but the effects of aging had been much more pronounced on him, much more grey. Dressed in beige he painted, his weary gaze coming to rest alternately on his model and his opus, with the glimmer of distressed astonishment that one might get from a knockout. Presently immobile, he held his brush at the ready. Chopin stopped behind him: in painstaking strokes, the watercolor depicted the hotel facade with its tall glass doors and rows of closed windows, with a level of detail that presupposed hours of care. No doubt installed there since morning, the artist had surely missed none of the comings and goings of the guests, who often paused near his station, throwing a critical gaze on his work and a supervisory glance at the facade before moving on.

Chopin did not move on. Exactly ten seconds passed, then the other man came to life: nimbly dipping his brush in color, in several strokes he opened one of the windows on the first floor; for an instant a reflection of daylight even zigzagged on its pane. Then in the opening appeared a furtive, mobile, rapidly sketched figure, a brief intrusion of cartoon into still life, who almost immediately disappeared back into a black circle, like Loopy the Loop and Woody Woodpecker at the end of the episode (*That's all, folks!*). Time to change color, and in three new strokes the casement closed up again, the facade regained its watercolor calm, and nothing had happened. Chopin let ten more seconds pass, then walked back up toward the hotel with hardly a glance for the window in which, under Mouezy-Eon's voluble fingers, the effigy of Vital Veber had just stirred. Now, to work.

The yellow hair had not moved from the groove on the closet, from which Chopin pulled his trunk. The interior of this luggage was cloistered into compartments: twelve lively young flies fluttered in a grillwork cube, with as many larvae squirming at the bottom of another cube made of Plexiglas. Various cavities contained fine pointed tools, several tubes and flasks, and stocks of infinitesimal electronic components, while three larger habitations harbored a hi-fi receiver with built-in recorder, a microscope, and a frontal scialytic lamp. Having washed his hands, Chopin unpacked his equipment, passed his flies in review, and selected three robust subjects.

The difficult thing was to grasp the insect, but once it was caught, turned over, and squeezed under the microscope's lens, once the motor muscles of its wings and legs were inhibited by mesothoracic pressure, it was child's play for Chopin to graft a microphone onto its metasternum, well centered between its halteres—no more complicated than adjusting the radar thirty years earlier, evenings after school, on a model Messerschmidt or Spitfire at 1:72 scale.

Once fitted out, the flies heavily returned to their cages, in somersaults, rebounds, clearly stunned by postoperative shock. Two of them, having first stayed still awhile to get used to this new ballast, finally took off again, reeducating themselves by flying in brief curves, then gradually reconstituting their habitual broken trail in the air. The third one did not get up; after attempting a few stimulations, miniature cardiac massages, Chopin recovered the mike from its corpse before isolating the two more resistant subjects, each one now in its individual cell to prevent them from coupling and screwing up the system. Then he looked up florists in the phone book, the nearest one being in Valenton. Just as he sometimes watched movies on television simply to see Marianne introduce them, so Chopin also procured, in a small newsstand at the entrance to Valenton, a fashion magazine in which Carole published her photos. Marianne, frozen the moment she leaves the studio's floodlights; Carole, who thrusts out her glass and cries, *Champagne!* the instant she leaves hers: is either the one Chopin truly wants? Is it with one or the other pressed against him that he could visit his parents, whom he hasn't seen in twenty years? No, no, no.

The round trip to Valenton took him two hours. Coming from the florist's, Chopin acquired a roll of blue masking tape at the stationer's. Then he lunched on a ham and butter sandwich at the bar of a corner café, leafing through his magazine near a young fellow and a tall bleached woman who envisioned life after death from an aperitif perspective: "Reincarnation," the young guy summarized, "isn't for the birds." All alone at the back of the room, a deaf-mute soliloquized in his sign language, discreetly moving his fingers between his legs beneath the table. Familiar with the most common codes, Chopin understood that the man was hashing over a marital problem, then one having to do with family allocations, complicated by a matter of back pay.

Returning to the hotel, Chopin shut himself in his room for two more hours to perfect his system, then went back down to take a walk. It was getting on to the end of the afternoon. Already the first drinks were being ordered at the bar, at the back of which, before a saucerful of peanuts and two mineral waters, the general secretary's bodyguards were seated. Chopin instantly identified them as such.

Fourteen

Being the general secretary's bodyguard was of course not the first mission for Perla Pommeck, nor for Rodion Rathenau. They were hardly beginners. Blonde with very dark-colored eyebrows, the fruit of a comfortable biotope, Perla had spent the first seventeen years of her life on the chic beaches of various internal seas. Elected Miss Sebastopol by plebiscite in August 1980, she had been recruited as of October by the special services that trained her in, for starters, turning around ambassadorial factotums. Her aptitudes as a vamp proving to be imperfect, they retrained her one year later in close-protection techniques by means of intensive workouts seasoned with anabolics. Her language was fairly crude.

For his part, Rathenau owed his career to compensation for a childhood handicap. Born prematurely, soon the victim of severe avitaminosis, so frail and rickety that at school they had considerately nicknamed him B-12, he swore as of adolescence to develop his musculature beyond all proportion. At that point, kinesitherapists and sports coaches became his only mentors, until he had acquired a morphology of steel. Alas, once he had entered the world of information, his bosses did not find it necessary to modify his old nickname, deeming to Rodion's utter despair that B-12 constituted a code name altogether in keeping with the institution's style.

Having avoided them, Chopin left the Parc Palace and skirted the main building toward the golf course, crossing the green toward the lake. Two boats occupied a minuscule cove defined by five yards of landing pier: a midget outboard, the square root of the Chris Craft, and a small ferry bordered with rope hand-rails, with benches bolted to the deck under a striped canopy. Beyond, reflected in the lake, the grey and the white vessels from the nearby airport followed each other into the sky, each in its continuous corridor.

Chopin remained there for barely fifteen minutes, then before returning to his room he turned back toward the hotel: poplars masked the back of the building up to the second floor, above which he spotted the window to his room. And on the first floor, in the workroom set up the evening before at the cryptanalyst's, Vital Veber had just closed the fat northeast file:

"That'll do for today," he sighed, "that's enough. I can't do any more. How about if the two of us go raise a glass?"

The cryptanalyst nodded while gathering up the scattered documents. Then they crossed the hall toward Veber's suite, the latter immediately sinking into a chair while the other prepared the drinks. His eyes closed, the general secretary seemed really tired; his entire body weighed on the armrest, and he held the roots of his nose between two fingers. There was a knock at the door.

"Be a good fellow and see who that is," said Veber without raising his eyelids.

It was a red-and-gold bellboy hidden behind an enormous bouquet, an alleluia of purple gladioli squeezed into a waterproof and saccular cellophane case, which a large ribbon held shut with a complicated knot. The twists and spirals of the ribbon fell in ringlets like curls, rustling with excessive flourish. Veber opened one eye and asked what was that, who was it for.

"Mister Veber," said the bellboy.

"Is there a card?"

The cryptanalyst had seized the bouquet; he pivoted it around while saying no, no card.

"Send it back," said Veber in a weary voice. "On second thought, no, leave it, I'll take care of it. It'll relax me. Here, just put it there. But we'll need a vase or something, won't we?"

The bellboy returned with a vase, a simple truncated crystal cone that he went to fill at the bathtub faucet while Veber undid the bouquet's wrapping, liberating the two special envoys from Chopin, who immediately tried to reap the soundtrack. Hands behind his back, the cryptanalyst watched him. "Did you see the fly?" he said. "The what," Veber said distractedly while deploying the gladioli in a bundle. "No, no." Then he planted the bouquet in the vase and stabilized it with asparagus shoots. Two floors above, headphones glued to his ears, Chopin was pleased to hear that the flowers were to his liking.

When the cryptanalyst had left, the general secretary emptied his glass and washed up a bit before slipping on a double-breasted smoking jacket, held shut by a rope belt and lined with flannel, over a scarf knotted like a jabot. He came and went in the room, back arched, hands in his jacket pockets. As the latter were sewn a bit too high, his elbows jutted out on either side of his inflated torso like atrophied wings or penguin flippers. For the moment, Chopin recorded nothing of great interest: eyedropper and tooth-brush noises, sigh, brief interjections.

Vital Veber stopped in front of the window and opened it, as several hours earlier he had been painted doing by Mouezy-Eon, whom he noticed, moreover, without paying him much attention: the watercolorist had not left his post below the terrace, obstinately reproducing the hotel down to the last glimmers of daylight. Chopin heard the slight creaking of the casement, and shortly afterward entirely different ambient sounds—breath of wind, song of bird, silence of altitude—confirmed his fears: escaped from Veber's room as soon as the latter had opened the window, the flies were now transmitting live from the hotel grounds. Swearing softly between his teeth, Chopin removed his headphones, put away his equipment, and went down to the bar to have a drink like everyone else.

Past the lobby and just before the entrance to the bar stretched a space with no precise vocation, which in earlier times must have been designated a smoking lounge. A dozen or so paintings were exhibited there, each the work of a different painter and each representing the Parc Palace du Lac, in its entirety or in detail: not only the facade but also the winter garden, a corner of the terrace, part of a wall. Among them, Chopin quickly recognized, by its scrupulous manner, an unknown work by Mouezy-Eon. The frame was brand-new, the paint scarcely dry; it had not been there long. A shadowy window in the rear of the building had particularly engaged the artist's inspiration. Chopin committed it to memory before entering the bar.

A mature pianist officiated, permanented to the millimeter, foundationed and lacquered by the spoutful. Rich deposit of false pearls and teeth, she was husking the refrain of "September Song" when he entered. Two of the nabobs spotted that morning on the terrace were drinking Pimm's at the bar with their secretaries, and at the back of the room Rodion Rathenau still sat, grafted to the same seat, getting fat on peanuts and irrigating himself with plain water. Chopin took a seat not far from the nabobs, seizing a few snatches of their conversation ("Oh, really? She left her American?") while detailing the leather and waxed-wood furniture. On the walls, antique engravings depicted English horses, Tarbes halfbreeds, Orloff trotters, and on the other side of the bar were polished, sheened, varnished accessories that the immaculate bartenders manipulated sacerdotally. It was restful; the music was restful. Chopin ordered a Bronx.

After the fourth Pimm's it was time to go dine. The glasses had been emptied of their contents, the bar of its. It was now appropriate to compile an initial report for Colonel Seck.

An hour later, therefore, the Karmann Ghia came to a halt on the corner of rues Lafayette and Bleue, before a phone booth. It was mainly a commercial neighborhood, and night-life was all but nonexistent. There were few lights in the windows after eight o'clock and few passers-by, other than a handful of European tourists who were drunk and glad to finally find their way back to the hotel. Chopin entered the booth. Through its glass walls, he inspected both ends of Rue Lafayette, as if to be sure that no one would see him lift the receiver. Except that he didn't lift it: he dialed Suzy Clair's number only with his eyes. Pulling the roll of blue masking tape from his pocket, he promptly tore off a square which he stuck to the underside of the telephone before leaving the booth.

One hundred yards from there was a small movie house showing *Forbidden Planet,* a film loved by Chopin and made in 1956 by Fred MacLeod Wilcox; he would just have time for a quick bite before the ten o'clock showing. In a nearby tavern he ordered a Bass with a couple of frankfurters, whose firm casings, synthetic like nylon, produced disturbing squeaks as they tore between his teeth.

So Chopin saw *Forbidden Planet* again, in which one could notably see a tiger being disintegrated in mid-leap, graceful in freshly-invented technicolor. Leaving the cinema, he looped by the phone booth before returning to his car. Searching with his fingertips under the apparatus, he found the square of masking tape, smoother and warmer than the metal. He unstuck it with the edge of his fingernail and looked at it: its color had changed. Confirming reception of the blue square following the habitual code, this one's yellow tone indicated that the colonel would meet, tonight, same time same place as before.

On the road home, Chopin kept the yellow square distractedly glued to his fingertip, poking at it like a flap of dead skin or an old Band-Aid. And in his room at the Parc Palace it seemed upon inspection that two more flies had passed away. As the larvae had not yet matured, the problem of relays would surely arise.

Fifteen

Parked before the carrion pavilion three hours later, Chopin did not wait this time for the Opel door to open for him: he climbed directly in. But in place of Colonel Seck, another man was sitting at the wheel, patiently leafing through a magazine of puzzles; Chopin immediately recognized the veteran Fernandez, reassigned from the expiatory chapel to the officer's car. With a cap in place of his kepi, his guardian's uniform made a very becoming chauffeur's outfit, patience being the lot of both professions. The car radio was on.

"The colonel went out for a moment," said Fernandez, indicating the pavilion. "He's in there. He won't be long."

"Fine," said Chopin. "I'll wait."

As on the other night, men passed by from time to time to empty out their split skulls and dismembered carcasses into tall containers: as before, Fernandez watched over bones.

"So," went Chopin. "No more Square Louis XVI?"

"An old buddy was looking around," Fernandez explained. "The colonel was good enough to lift a finger. He's very good, the colonel; he took me with him. My buddy took over for me, over there."

At this hour, the radio broadcast nothing more than a few confidences in hushed tones from desperate listeners: at the other end of the line, the throaty-voiced announcer was a mother to them, always seeming about to dispense perverse advice. "Well," said Chopin, "I'm going to see what he's doing." He left the car and walked toward the pavilion entrance.

Past the airtight plastic portcullis, the infernal tumult of guts suddenly burst forth: dozens of men with red and white faces, in black and white dress, called to each other while cutting muscles, severing tendons, and sculpting viscera, shouting numbers around their stalls stuffed with barrels of livers, bags of hearts to be captured, seminaries of brains, crowds of feet, lines of tongues wagging in the void, lungs by the shovelful and kidneys galore, quintals of sweetmeats, tons of lights, masses of spleens, and trillions of red cheeks marked with a green stamp. Chopin looked around for the tall, dark silhouette of Colonel Seck amid all that, then began to cross the building lengthwise.

From up close, the tripe butchers did not look feverish; they didn't even especially seem to be working—they calmly chatted about organs among themselves, designated the ones they were exposing, evaluated them, compared them, removed them, picked one up now and again to cut in half, just to see. Occasionally someone passed and uttered a figure; the blink of an eye and it's a done deal. This is how instantly business is handled.

At the end of the pavilion, shockwaves emitted strongly from the skull-crushing stalls, distributed via a short network of corridors. That is where Chopin found Colonel Seck in conversation with a Malian skull-crusher on the threshold of his work area, near a tall can of steaming liquid. The colonel seemed in fine fettle, completely at ease in the commerce of debrained skulls. "This is Mr. Touré," he said, "who breaks heads. We've just met." His interlocutor smiled, dressed in a black outfit and very high white boots; his coat of mail shone in moiré wavelets on his chest.

The boxer-pianist's hand that he held out to Chopin was equally gloved in iron.

Colonel Seck explained that emptying sheep's heads of their brains was Mr. Touré's profession, the latter having in fact offered to show how he works, his tools, the whole business, but unfortunately, the colonel lamented, we have some matters to see to in the immediate. We'll be back.

"So?" he asked as soon as they were outside the pavilion.

"I didn't get much," admitted Chopin. "The sound quality wasn't very clear, and in any case Veber opened the window and naturally they flew right out." (The colonel winced.) "I told you that would happen, didn't I? I warned you. Anyway, I'll try to plant a few more in his room tomorrow, but I think he spends most of his time in the other suite, with the cryptanalyst. I know where it is now, thanks to Mouezy-Eon."

"Ah, yes," the colonel nodded. "Mouezy-Eon. So you saw his painting?"

"Of course," said Chopin.

"It's good, what he does," judged the colonel. "Don't you think? I find it has real charm. Real talent. Did you know he sculpts, too?"

"Uh, no," said Chopin.

"For years I've been encouraging him to exhibit, but that Mouezy-Eon is terrible, he's never ready. I mean, I'm not saying a gallery right off the bat, of course not, but maybe a restaurant, for instance, I don't know, or a small shopping mall to start with. Even banks—my branch near Wagram did it for a pastel artist. Well, anyway. Would you like to take a walk?"

They strolled for a moment on one edge of the circular avenue, on the other side of which, twenty-four hours a day, glassed-in restaurants displayed their wares at all angles, like an aquarium. Without hearing them, one could see people laughing, ordering, shouting as if the sound had been cut, or as if in a three-dimensional drive-in showing a silent film for rows of empty vans and blind tractor-trailers. Two tall buildings dominated the area: the ice factory and the central administration tower, which was barely visible in the nocturnal fog over the northern entrance. Every floor of the tower was dark except for the last. Continuous shift of mustache on cigarette butt, a plainclothes policeman watched—also twenty-four hours a day—over his own screens: entrances and exits to and from the national food market, as well as its intersections and sensitive areas, not the least of these being the safes and vaults of the twenty-four banks aligned beneath his feet.

As he walked, the colonel rummaged in his suit: from out the mother-of-pearl lining of his breast pocket emerged the silhouette of a Montecristo no. 2, whose end he clipped with his keyring scissors. He moistened it while nostalgically pondering the sky pierced by the Paris-Niamey flight; then to light it, he sat on the running board of a fifteen-ton truck.

"Getting back to business," he said, exhaling a long stratus, "it seems that Veber is going to have a visitor. Perhaps tomorrow night. If you could keep an eye out."

"Do we know who?"

"Not really. A woman, I believe."

"It figures he'd have a girl brought in," Chopin judged. "He *is* on vacation, after all."

The colonel shook his head while continuing to smoke. Still standing, Chopin pondered the fifteen-tonner. There were, in fact, girls everywhere in the driver's cab: remarkable pinup photos, drawings, pennants, statuettes, and decals, bikini-clad in the worst of cases. The one painted on the door above the colonel's head, dressed only in tight-fitting boots and a fringed bolero, straddled, face forward, an Electroglide motorcycle, the wind from the ride holding said bolero open: unique breasts and eternal lips, it would surely be such a girl that Veber would have visit him. As general secretary, one could procure these unreal creatures without the slightest difficulty.

"Is it really worth recording that?" Chopin pointed out. "What could be more predictable than a fuck-tape?"

"I'm not sure," the colonel said while getting up. "You never know. Send one or two flies out all the same, just to see."

They began walking again. Leaving the meat zone, then the fruits and vegetables, they skirted smaller warehouses brimming with various foodstuffs, generalized pavilions in which the whole-sale trade feels the pull of the retail. As they noticed Fernandez at the back of one of them quietly negotiating the purchase of foie gras, the colonel grumbled, rushed up to his new driver, and confiscated the organ with forceful admonishments. The distinct shouts of his case officer made Chopin nervous.

"We could be a bit more discreet, don't you think?"

They headed back toward the cars. Fernandez walked five yards ahead of them, pouting, head sunk into his shoulders.

"Never fear, nothing to worry about," smiled Colonel Seck as he made the foie gras jump in the hollow of his large hand. "We've got it made here like papa in mama."

"I don't mean for me," Chopin specified, "I mean you. Some-one could spot you, recognize you."

"You mean because I'm black?" the colonel speculated.

Chopin shrugged a third of shoulder.

"We'll meet again on Thursday," the officer informed him. "Thursday at noon. Mouezy-Eon will let you know where. If you have any problems before then, blue tape Rue Bleue phone booth, got it? What year is your car, by the way? You don't see too many like that."

After the Opel had left, Chopin inspected one of the containers stuffed with yellowish bones fringed with coalescing red and white scraps: armored in colors of ultramarine, emerald, or smoke, depending on their branch of service, squadrons of meat flies patrolled the locale at all hours. Chopin leaned over, remaining perfectly immobile for six seconds without breathing; then sudden as a cramp his right hand sliced through the impure air and six seconds later his left opened the Karmann Ghia's door. Already his closed fist was itching from within, the new elements drumming against his palm and the inner joints of his fingers. The glove compartment still contained a small cage of fine brass wire, and Chopin counted as he put the flies in it, one after the other, as if into a corral. Seven in one shot: not bad.

Sixteen

Softened by the double tulle-stitch curtains and the double bullet-proof windows, daylight entered affectionately into Maryland's office. Eyes shining, features drawn by the lack of sleep, Colonel Seck recounted his night.

"Anyway, I'll see him again on Thursday," he concluded. "To be honest, I haven't quite figured out where. Not far from that hotel, in any case—always the same area."

A valet had just appeared, bearing an opulent brunch on a vermilion tray, which he posed on a low table between them. In one motion, Maryland snared three precocious little strawberries which he messily gobbled in a single bite. The colonel paused, unsympathetically watching the pink thread that dribbled from the corner of the other man's mouth. Ever scrupulous about his appearance, he disapproved as much of these mediocre manners as he did of the chronic presence of ash stains—at best—on the upper functionary's perpetually wrinkled grey suit. That wasn't what *he* would look like, if their positions were reversed.

"Maybe the large cemetery next door," he resumed. "It's fairly quiet during the week."

"Your choice," Maryland swallowed. "Are you really sure about this fellow?"

"My word," said Seck, sizing up the scrambled eggs, "he hasn't served very often, it's true. But that's not a problem, he's really not bad. And besides, all in all, he's mainly there as window dressing."

The telephone rang very discreetly. Maryland answered it, said that it was no for Japan, then crushed his yellow Gauloise before buttering himself a scone. "So what exactly can he do?" he persisted.

"Lots of little things," the colonel assured him. "You'd be amazed. He's a scientist, but don't be fooled, he's also very resourceful. You can't imagine how good he is with his fingers."

Having downed his milky tea with an abrupt gesture, creating a second, beige dribble from the other corner of his mouth, Maryland settled an impassive eye on the officer.

"And are you still planning to leave once the operation's over?"

"I've always been loyal to the service, as you know," the colonel recalled. "But it doesn't keep me from having my convictions, as you also know. Of course I'm leaving. In any case, it's good for the operation; this way the main thing will go unnoticed. And besides, at least there it'll be easier to go to Africa as often as I want."

Maryland produced a skeptical grimace while spreading way too much marmalade on his crust of bread.

"As you like. So long as we're not shortchanged."

"It should go all right," said Colonel Seck. "You can count on me."

At around noon the colonel left the Ministry, his eyes still smarting a bit, but feeling strong, sure, and master of himself. This planned departure clearly appealed to him. There was just one thing, which was that he wanted to win or lose a bit more money, after all, before changing scenery. So he got into his car and murmured the order to Fernandez, who was ready to drop, to take him to Rue Héliopolis, to the green room of a private games club. This is a club that many people frequent night and day: dark men with tight-fitting tuxedos and slicked hair, blonde women with distant gazes and low-cut backs. The clientele always displays complete seriousness; the only ones who smile, rarely and ferociously, are occasional staff members—croupiers not included.

Past the velvet doors, the colonel skirted two little craps tables. To the other side of the bar they were busy with chemin de fer and baccarat; a roulette wheel hummed in a farther corner, and boule in a larger corner. Having chosen his table in the green room, composed of the tenor Fred Vauvenargues and Karlheinz Schumann, a well-known seducer and professional player, with a big chemical industrialist from the Bouches-du-Rhône in the role of pigeon, he ordered a glass of champagne and a new deck. It was Vauvenargues's deal.

I like hesitating over the fate of cards, thought Colonel Seck. I enjoy turning them over, and how I love to lay them down. But there he banished his self-contentment: the lyrical artist having just dealt him a passably sterile hand with no pair, the least he could do was concentrate. Above his head, a sign reminded everyone that those playing poker were requested to maintain SILENCE.

Seventeen

Meanwhile, Chopin looked after the fresh set of flies, choosing the most able-bodied by the vigor of their beating wings—identified as a sign of joy by Abbé Pioger back in 1822—and implanting little microphones on them.

In late morning, the hotel's floors were empty, paced only by the chambermaids; their voices sounded loud in the moist chaos of rooms still misty with emanations of soap, wax, and breathing. They aired them out, erased the intimacy of rumpled beds. Down the hallways they pushed their carts in crews of three, chain-cleaning several rooms at once, one assigned to the sheets and the other to the facilities, with the third holding the vacuum cleaner by its leash.

Those on the first floor were about to attack the sector that included Veber's suite, and Chopin, who was following at a distance, stepped back quickly when he saw Perla Pommeck planted at one end of the corridor, whose other end must have been guarded by Rathenau. Huddled in a recess, invisible to the pair of gorillas, he continued to observe the chambermaids' technique, movement by movement and sheet by sheet, trying to spot in the pile of linens those that came from Veber's bed—close enough to hear their comments as well:

"William's a funny guy," the vacuum cleaner was notably expounding. "He doesn't want to be a store clerk anymore. He says,

'I don't want to be a store clerk anymore.'"

"William is unstable, Vero, and you know it," diagnosed her sister colleague's voice, amplifed from the hollow of the bathtub.

Vero pouted, then revved her machine. Chopin sneaked away, knowing what he needed to know.

He spent almost an hour in a deck chair by the lake. On the opposite shore, which holds a recreational park, he noticed the silhouettes of fishermen patiently waiting for bream and black bass, even though the water seemed fairly synthetic, too clean and too cold to be inhabited; an unsettled wind made changing platelets run over its surface the way a finger plays over velvet. Slicing the water diametrically came the little ferry that twice daily made the crossing: guests of the Parc Palace were sitting under the red-and-white striped canopy, and on the front bench, turned toward them, an accordionist released bunches of demisemiquavers that skippingly floated over the surface of the water, making points at the crests of the wavelets. Clinging one to the other following the wind's random trajectory, the notes did not necessarily reach Chopin in the order recommended by the sheet music.

In the evening, after dinner, he made the acquaintance of Dr. Belsunce, a lively, walleyed man who had a bottle with his name on it. His ample petroleum blue suit and his navy bow tie that also hung loose seemed to have been stolen from the vestiaries of dance contest orchestras, and the green ribbon in his buttonhole commemorated nothing that Chopin knew of. Behind his heavy-framed glasses, only his very sharp right eye—severe or waggish, depending—remained fixed on you, while his left alighted elsewhere, stamped with an expression of candid, confident, absent patience, like a distracted spouse who would never listen to what the doctor ordered.

Dietician in his soul, general practitioner by necessity, Belsunce had been a sometime guest of the Parc Palace, back when. Then he had done a few favors, dried some head colds, relieved a couple of sprains, fine-tuned diets, and prescribed substances listed under *Narcotics*. Observing that his thinning charisma worked without much loss of revenue on the overstuffed matrons with overstuffed bank accounts, the hotel management had ended up offering him the job of resident physician, turning the room next to his into a consulting chamber. The doctor treated in the afternoon, devoting his mornings to perfecting a new stroke in the Parc Palace swimming pool. And in the evening, at the bar, he emptied his bottle in the company of his opulent, Alexandra-saturated patients.

Chopin kept the doctor company for a moment, long enough for the latter to tell a bit of his life story, their four elbows aligned on the bar. The overripe pianist from teatime had been replaced by an organist of similar age, whose russet toupee slipped a notch and in the same direction as his spirited movements, and one of his contact lenses sometimes fell on the keyboard of the Hammond organ: without skipping a kneaded beat, he sought his missing lens between two black keys, quickly spat on it, and glued it back to his cornea.

Back up in his room, Chopin laid out his insects and his equipment, then began constructing two small spheric cages from iron wire and card stock: the size of agate marbles, held closed by simple pressure, they opened when pressure was released. In order to feel a little less alone, he had turned on the television, selecting a placid documentary about butterflies in Southern China. The latter, it seemed, had it made: the voice-over made it sound as if no fate was sweeter than being a bombyx in Formosa. Absorbed in his labors, Chopin was not really following the broadcast, leaving his caged flies to watch it alone, as guys in prison might watch girls on the California beaches.

The following morning, Chopin found himself, as the day before at the same hour, following the cleaning women, happy to have from Vero some fresh news of William ("So *I* said to him, I said, William, if you could see the way you talk to me"). While they cleaned the final rooms preceding the bodyguarded hallway, he quietly approached a laundry cart, made a quick calculation, and slipped his little cages between the folds of the sheets that should have been destined for the general secretary. Immediately afterward Chopin returned to his room, ordered room service, and donned his headphones: having returned to his own after a morning of work at the cryptanalyst's, Vital Veber had also ordered something to his taste: hefty pickles in an hors d'oeuvres dish, cold cuts under a glass bell, hot cabbage, black radishes, soda water.

The general secretary ate distractedly while holding himself very straight, as if he were envisioning a lofty objective. From his chair he pondered the rain outside, which was now falling on the grounds. With an absent air, he shooed away a little blonde crumb fallen on his sleeve; a small grey fly landed on the sausage. Suspended above him on an arm of the chandelier, a larger fly with cobalt blue thorax watched with all his ocelli to make sure the general secretary didn't overly brutalize his colleague, currently huddled behind the pastrami.

Guided by a sound engineer's instinct, the two insects had divided the labor, the blue capturing the room's overall ambience and the grey sticking as close as possible to Veber—from whom Chopin, in any case, did not hear anything particularly pertinent:

chewing, swallowing, occasional burp, clack of the tongue like an on-off switch or a few words unconsciously uttered in the wake of his thoughts, the way the rolling sea sometimes for an instant thrusts a bar of reefs into the open. Whispered words, mumbled in a language unfamiliar to Chopin; distant childhood from a vast, glacial province.

Then came the silence of coffee, visited by a lapping of suction; then several minutes of digestive silence; then, after the sound of footsteps indicated that Veber had gone into his bedroom, the silence of a nap sawed through by rippling snores. Chopin loosened the lightweight vise of his headphones and left them straddling the back of a chair. Leaving the recorder on as a safety precaution, he, too, stretched out on his bed after having cast a glance out the window: in the distance, the wind and rain were making the lake boil.

They awoke at the same moment, resumed their labors at the same time: in a rustle of papers leafed through for two hours without a word, Vital Veber worked. Ensconced in an easy chair, crossed legs dangling over the armrest, Chopin listened to him work. Once the telephone rang for the general secretary, who picked up and said yes, right away, very well; shortly afterword there was a knock on his door. Chopin turned up the sound and heard another voice, no doubt the cryptanalyst's, speaking about a file, about the absence in this file of a synthesis or about the lack of a synthesis of a file—it wasn't very clear. The flies must have been prolonging their own siesta in a far-off corner.

"It's possible," said Veber, rustling a new sheet of paper. "Try with this, perhaps."

"All right," went the voice. "I'll see how it goes."

A pause: for several instants more, Chopin heard only the rain falling unevenly, covering the cryptanalyst's muffled voice, in sudden squalls alternating with brief periods of calm, as if emptied from a bag by someone up above—from the rhythm of its falling, one could easily imagine the movement of the arms shaking the bag. "No," Veber finally said, "this evening I'll be dining downstairs." Chopin nodded his head.

At eight o'clock sharp, in the middle of the empty dining room, Dr. Belsunce was sitting alone before a round plate with rare beef on it, his daily paper folded in a square next to him. His sharp right eye deciphered the news while his left one calmly watched over the beef. From a distance, one of them noticed Chopin and Belsunce waved him over, indicating a free table setting just opposite him. Chopin approached, casting a circular glance around the dining room; its back wall, made entirely of glass, looked out on the terrace, where in summer one could eat outdoors.

"I'm afraid I won't be dining until later," he apologized. "I have a few things to do beforehand. I'm sorry. Perhaps tomorrow, if you'd like. Is that all right?"

"This sauce doesn't mean a thing," the doctor judged. "In any case, you know me, anything with red meat…"

Having taken his leave, Chopin dallied awhile in the lobby. Near the doors, a bellboy was helping a vast client on with her fur: though standing on tiptoes, he proceeded with suppleness and savoir-faire, as if he were setting up a tent and diapering an infant at the same time. And in the smoking lounge were several new works, mostly portraits of unknown persons, painted by unknown persons. Indubitably in the manner of Mouezy-Eon, only one of the watercolors represented an inanimate place, a life all the more still in that it depicted an alignment of tombstones: one could read on the most imposing one the name of King Zog the First of Albania. Chopin nodded then and there and left the smoking lounge. The solid matron had finally found the entrance to the last sleeve of her mink; her hand reemerged at the other end, miraculously clenching a banknote to the bellhop's great delight.

An hour later, the dining room was filled. Discreetly posted near the double door, Chopin inventoried the diners. In two days, most of them had become familiar to him, except for one that he knew only by ear. But he identified him all the same: sitting at the far end of the room, his back to the picture window, the general secretary was facing his way.

Veber looked just as he did on his book jackets, but the expression on his face was less tragic, less historic, banalized by smiles and light conversation. And he was smiling enormously, the least one can do when trying to woo a young lady sitting across from you, who was dressed in an advantageous yellow bodice and whom Chopin, from his vantage point, could see only from behind. The shoulders of the yellow-clad woman remained still; evidently she was scarcely reacting to her companion's courtly proposals, general secretary or no. That's right, Chopin reasoned, these guys hire girls so expensive that they don't even laugh, that they feign haughty indifference: ardent igloos, they seem inaccessible, the better to exercise their art.

It wasn't altogether necessary to learn more about this, perhaps, but what one wouldn't do to make the colonel happy. Chopin left his observation post, crossed the lobby, and went out. Outside he ran under the rain, swearing as he rounded the hotel toward its empty terrace; from the shadows he could observe the dining room in the other direction. He neared the picture window without at first being able to make out the girl's face, Veber's wide back masking his rental, his possession for an evening.

When a movement finally revealed her, Chopin stiffened and his entire body suddenly grew cold: Suzy, Suzy Clair *née* Moreno herself was sitting across from the general secretary. Chopin remained frozen for a few seconds, his mind equally frozen as the rain streamed over him. Then he remembered to breathe, to think, to wonder what was she doing there, what's going on here, and first of all, what's she doing wearing that awful yellow job, where did she get that yellow job?

Eighteen

Frozen under the black rain, Chopin watched them right up through dessert, forging hypotheses all the while. Veber spoke almost the entire time, whereas Suzy expressed little; only once did she smile, coldly. They seemed, in the final account, to be engaged in a serious talk, with no apparent strategy of seduction—but after they had risen from the table and left the dining room for the lobby, he still worried that they might be waiting together for the same elevator.

Chopin took the one after and ran to his room, where he rapidly towelled his hair dry before donning the headphones. Sitting on the edge of the bed, he grunted approvingly when he realized that Veber was alone. Nothing very interesting: running water and physiological noises; audaciously nearing the toothbrush glass, the grey fly managed an extreme close-up of the eyedropper. Veber heaved a great sigh as he lay back on the bed—the way guys in prison sigh, once the television has been switched off, while scratching one more notch in the wall's plaster—then textile scumblings preceded the click of the bedside lamp.

The next morning, Chopin did not leave his room for fear of running into Suzy, and especially in hopes of explaining her presence by listening in on Veber. Leaving the tape recorder running, he lay on his bed, eyes on the ceiling, ears in the general secretary's room, not moving other than to change the tape every hour and to camouflage his equipment when the bellboy brought more coffee. Flat on his back, Chopin counted the tricolored bouquets that were repeated along the wallpaper, on the chairs and curtains, the cushions and bedspread, everywhere. He counted them three times without ever arriving at the same result.

After twenty-four hours in service, the first fly to fall was the little grey whose job was to stick close to Veber, always in the front lines and therefore more intrusive, more threatened by gestures of annoyance, and especially by swats of the newspaper, a weapon singularly feared in France by the entire species since 1631. Heedless despite centuries of experience, the little grey found herself supremely exposed when she rested on the window, completely out in the open, a pure naive target on a clear field. Posted on his arm of the chandelier, the fat blue in charge of the ambience mike helplessly witnessed the demise of his colleague, whom Veber immolated against the cold pane with the help of an economics supplement folded lengthwise.

After the ambient fly had succumbed in turn, from cardiac arrest early that same afternoon, the mikes should in theory have continued to work for several more hours. But the location of one, stuck under the window between the wall and the radiator hood, did not allow for very good transmission; and Veber's heel had unwittingly pulverized the other, fallen into the tall wool shag in a vertical drop from the lighting fixture, waiting to be vacuumed up by Vero.

Chopin, temporarily laid off and bored with counting the bouquets on the wall, searched in his bags for the draft of a half-finished article devoted to the *Stilpon graminum,* a one-millimeter diptera that in the month of June frequents the entrances to waterways. He transcribed his notes more neatly in his off moments, began working without much conviction: as he continued to get stuck on the same sentence, he stood up an instant to stretch, went back to work, then got up again immediately afterward to fetch a glass of water or a beer from the minibar, pissing in the sink on the way, snapping on the TV only to snap it off again, glancing out the window toward the lake: spotting Suzy.

She was walking alone at the water's edge, a book in hand, still wearing that yellow bodice and a black skirt, which are also the colors of the *Stilpon*. Chopin's field glasses were powerful enough to detail the hem of her skirt, trembling in the mobile air of the seasonal cusp, but not enough to make out the book's title. After Suzy had disappeared toward the landing pier, he called the front desk, which informed him that Mrs. Clair had been occupying Suite 44 since the previous evening but that she was out for the moment. As his microphones had stopped transmitting information, which, moreover, was of no interest, it was doubly useless to wait. And besides, it was time to go.

The Karmann Ghia then crossed a slack suburban network of roads, not truly highways and not really streets. Brick and concrete, millstone and zinc defined obscure workshops, deserted bakeries, desperate lodgings. Abutting factories that produced sanitary facilities, batches of sinks and piles of bathtubs covered former working-class garden plots. Between the different town centers in which the skyscrapers and services gathered, it was not always clear to Chopin what plan held these agglomerations together.

The monumental approach to the Thiais cemetery leads to a large, complicated intersection of one-way side paths surrounded by construction scaffolds and service stations, empty lots and parking areas for industrial vehicles. The cemetery itself is a flat rectangle of 250 acres, which mainly harbors the ashes of the economically disadvantaged, though one can also find the victims of several air disasters, the passengers' tombs kept distinct from those of the crew, as well as the latest to be condemned to death, their heads buried apart from their bodies.

Loaded with wreckage, two semitrailers from the auto yard slowly maneuvered before the gateway. As soon as they had freed a passage, Chopin steered into the necropolis and took Avenue de l'Est, which he followed for about half a mile up to Division 89. He parked his car beneath the trees that bordered it, behind the colonel's Opel.

The latter, alone in the midst of the Division, seemed to be lost in thought before the mausoleum of Zog the First, a composition of pillars that framed a stela embossed with the royal emblem: a bicephalous winged creature. Chopin walked toward him while inspecting the environs: no one. Only several living winged creatures cast suspicious glances as he approached, some perched on badly-maintained tombs, others nervously extracting their worm from the rich humus. Among these birds, there were no sparrows, no pigeons (in which the area nonetheless abounded), not even a blackbird with too-vivid beak; only crows and ravens all in black, and occasionally an airborne magpie in half-mourning.

"So who was the woman?" asked Colonel Seck.

"No one," said Chopin. "A call girl, just as we thought."

"You'll let me have the tape, eh?" the colonel said in a casual tone.

"No problem," said Chopin, who owned many tapes of all sorts. Then he detailed what one could hear when Veber was alone:

nothing very useful, to tell the truth. Apart from a slight coughing fit here and there, the television at news time, and the hiss of pages from the economics supplements, there really was little to report. And a long phrase in a foreign tongue, propelled by a dream in the middle of the night, once, would not get them very far.

"You'll let me have *that* tape as well. We'll try to study it all the same. And the cryptanalyst?"

"Nothing," repeated Chopin. "All insignificant." He was careful to note the comings and goings of the two bodyguards, but refrained from mentioning Suzy, whose presence, as he saw it, did not concern the intelligence functionaries.

Before finding his way back out of the cemetery, he got lost near the common grave, a fallow field boasting no decorations apart from three plastic carnations, tossed flat on the ground; then again in the sector of body parts donated to science, which was indicated only by a marble plaque: several laboratories thanked seven acres of voluntary offal. He finally found the central artery. Night was about to fall. He returned to the Parc Palace du Lac.

Nineteen

AFTER A SHOWER, then dinner, which he had sent up, Chopin glanced at the surviving flies; but his heart wasn't in it. So he turned on the television, staring at it for almost three hours, forcing himself to watch carefully, not letting himself be distracted by other thoughts. If one really concentrates on an adventure of Mannix's, one eventually manages to follow the whole thing; it's even fairly easy if one puts one's mind to it. Cruising from one channel to the next, he then recognized the beginning of *Some Came Running*: a bus rolls through the countryside, carrying several passengers, among them Frank Sinatra asleep in his seat and wearing his army uniform. The bus stops in a small town; the driver turns around to Sinatra and calls out, "Hey, soldier! Soldier!" It was nearly midnight. Chopin, who seemed calm until then, jumped up, cut the volume on the set, grabbed the telephone, and asked for Suite 44. At the other end of the line, someone picked up on the first ring.

"It's me," said Chopin, and as Suzy didn't answer immediately he repeated that it was he, Franck. No doubt she would exclaim: Is that you? But, where are you? How did you know that I? And in fact, that was what she said, except in a hushed voice.

"I'm right nearby," answered Chopin. "One floor down. I'll explain. I have to see you."

"No," Suzy whispered sharply. "You can't. How did you know I was here?"

"I'll explain," Chopin repeated. "I'm coming to see you."

"No," she cut him off. "Please don't. I mean it."

"I'll be right there," Chopin specified.

"I won't open up."

"Then *I* will," said Chopin. "*I'll* open up."

He hung up and immediately stood, searched in his trunk for a fat ring bearing a hundred passkeys. These he rapidly picked through, recalling the composite portrait of the ones hanging behind the front desk. Very quickly he found its homologue, then left the room while Shirley MacLaine stepped off the bus, fur over one arm, and came running after Frank Sinatra.

Along the hallway up to the stairs, the aligned doors were like empty closets. Chopin began climbing the thickly carpeted steps, in the thick silence aggravated by a muffled, distant music, no doubt coming from the bar and almost unrecognizable in the stairwell, half-heard like the buzzing of the night light in a hospital corridor. Taking the stairs two at a time, Chopin felt the noise of his body like a running orchestra, his heart a bass drum, his breathing a studded cymbal, and maracas for his joints. He marked a pause in front of number 44, an instant of fear or scruple, before fishing the passkey out of his pocket. Then he silently opened the door, entered, and closed it behind him.

At first glance, all was dark, unoccupied. No lamp shone. Only a television in the far corner provided a little moving clarity. Profiles of slender armchairs framed a low table; a large mirror on the wall doubled their shadows. Letting his eyes adjust, Chopin understood that 44 was an L-shaped suite, located at the corner of the facade and composed of two rooms at right angles. The television was installed in this corner, facing the other room, which was invisible from the entry. On its screen, Sinatra, now dressed in civvies, was settling with Shirley MacLaine into Dean Martin's place, where all three of them began to drink copiously.

Chopin quietly unglued himself from the door, trying not to knock into the furniture, creeping toward the television as Dean Martin got into the bathtub without removing his hat. When he reached the television, he turned toward the other room, which was filled by a large white bed. "I told you not to come," Suzy calmly reminded him from the shadows.

Chopin could make out almost nothing of her in the bed, except her eyes reflecting the TV screen, her bare arm under the sheet. As he approached, she whispered, "No, you have to leave," and as he continued to approach she thrust the remote control out at him, her hand closed over the box as if on a handgun. But he kept coming under the little machine's rays, indestructible, as the monsters in the films of Fred MacLeod Wilcox are unfazed by the most potent lasers. When Suzy laughed softly and dropped her guard, Chopin leaned over and touched his fingers to her shoulder, the back of her neck; she opened her arms, then the sheets.

Up to the end of the film they lay close, holding each other without speaking, except when Chopin again wanted to know what this was all about, what was going on, and Suzy told him I'll explain tomorrow, I'll tell you everything. Tomorrow. Now you really have to go. As they were kissing one last time, *Some Came Running* ended in a cemetery more inviting than the one in Thiais; Chopin got up during the closing credits. Passing back in front of the TV, he encountered Marianne, all smiles on the screen, who announced a broadcast of *Undercurrent* for the following week as part of the ongoing retrospective. She wished him an excellent night.

He then found himself back in the dark hallway, but once the door was shut behind him he barely had time to walk a foot before a powerful fist grabbed him by the shoulder and pinned him solidly to the wallpaper, while someone pressed a small hollow cylinder between his shoulder blades.

"Let's go," Rathenau's voice breathed in his ear. "Just like in the movies. Up against the wall and hands on your head."

Having done so, Chopin sensed an aroma of eau de cologne drifting toward him like a ghost, then immediately afterward a brief sting in the crook of his arm. It was a benign and relatively painless feeling, but three seconds later sound and image switched off and Chopin tripped into a coma. Welcome, Doctor Bong.

Twenty

CHOPIN CAME TO lying on his side, stuffed into the rear of a moving vehicle, in the position of an overturned penitent. An iron wire stretched across his back, linking the handcuffs that shackled ankles and wrists, permitted no more than the weak twitching of his fingers, toes, and face muscles. And the slight stinging near his elbow from the shot, which reminded him of the prick of the little deer fly *(Chrysops pictus),* the subject of a contribution that had been widely noted in its day,[*] was nothing next to the itching. Glued to his mouth from ear to ear, a large patch of duct tape kept him from complaining about the situation.

He established that the vehicle was a station wagon, whose rear was separated from the passenger compartment by a summary and solid grill, of the kind used by the owners of vicious dogs. From where he was, Chopin could see neither who was driving nor if there were any other occupants. Apart from the engine's four strokes, he heard nothing but a dashboard radio turned down low, hardly perceptible from where he was.

Since any stretching at all entailed deeper cuts in his wrists and ankles, Chopin hunched more tightly into himself to give his

---

[*] Bloch, J. B., Chopin, F., et al., "Notes Toward a Typology of Mouth Hooks in the Ectoparasites of Larger Domestic Vertebrates," *Bull. Soc. Exot. Path.,* XLVI: 3 (1983), pp. 64–109, 11 pl., 29 figs.

bonds a bit more slack. Flexing his neck, for an instant he caught several whiffs of Suzy's perfume from his clothes, which immediately dissipated in the classic aromas of gasoline, dust, and cold tobacco, with a brief underlying memory of new car smell. His cheek was pressed against the rough matting. Among the things in this trunk area that were not himself, he recognized, first off, the habitual denizens: ropes and oily rags, a jack, bungy cords, and a can of 10W50 motor oil. Through a fraction of window above him, day was breaking inside a triangular section of cloudy sky.

They must have been driving on the highway, given the smoothness of the ride and the particular variations of the surface coating, perceptible in the changes of sound produced by the tires: muffled exhalations, light tremblings. Sometimes a sharp organ note was held for miles at a stretch; sometimes the road texturing provoked small, regular jolts, as if the motor were prone to microscopic blackouts. In the triangle of sky, Chopin saw an airplane, birds, and the tops of overtaken trucks.

They were in fact driving on the southern highway toward Paris. Rathenau exited at Villejuif, taking Route Stratégique and skirting a large, bright pink ensemble before heading back toward the highway to turn into a small, inanimate artery that runs parallel to it. Halfway up this street, behind staggered cubes of boxwood, rose a three-story apartment house bordered by a narrow vegetal corridor, furnished with lawn tables and chairs blackened by soot, and watched over by an imputrescible cherub. It was evident that no one ventured out to take the air under that gaseous sky, in the fracas of highway onto which the apartment windows peered without further ado.

Rathenau cut the engine in the underground garage: silence

in the shadows, under the sweat of yellowish lamps. The station wagon's gate was lifted and Chopin again smelled Perla's eau de cologne as she leaned over him to remove the wire and take the handcuffs off his ankles; then Rathenau gripped his shoulders to yank him from the vehicle. At the back of the garage, punctuated by a neon line, a metal door led to an unadorned cement stairway. Solidly flanked by his kidnappers, Chopin began climbing the steps, their corners littered with bright red grains of rat poison, his eyes bulging above the duct tape.

They met no one on their way up to the second floor, where Rathenau promptly opened a door leading to an apartment that smelled stale; then they hustled Chopin toward a room that was more distinctly rank. They locked him inside after having freed his wrists, leaving him the job of skinning his own lips as he ripped off the tape. That done, he inspected the room.

It was minimally furnished: a mattress under a bedspread, the foam carcass of a chair, a mirrorless sink in one corner with a sky blue plastic potty seat beneath. Probably as a consequence of a leak in the pipes, the wallpaper was peeling off in sheets; its seams, maintained by a stitch of glue, hung from the wall like a slashed jacket, exhibiting margins dotted with blackish brown mold. Not a single hard, sharp, or pointed object could be found; nothing that would allow him to attack the window's double panes, thick as the ones on a presidential limo and offering as sole view the back of a soundproof wall meant to blot out the highway traffic.

Similarly, highways leave Paris via several exits, bordered by all kinds of soundproof walls, each very different from the others. Some of these walls undulate like mutant sheet metal, others deploy arches of piping; occasionally one suggests a souvenir of the blockhouse embellished with climbing vines. Topped with awnings, larded with bumps or buttresses, these works of art are fashioned from various materials: concrete, metal, plastic, ceramic or mirror, terra cotta and fire-treated wood. Inclined at varying angles over the roadways, some are also translucent or almost transparent, or even better, like this one, just pierced by glass portholes barely one yard in diameter. Between this wall and the building's facade, a narrow rectangle of vivacious weeds, of synthetic and shiny forest green, grew in the shadows.

Chopin retreated from the window and sat in the chair, then stretched out on the mattress. The pain in his ankles was fading less quickly than the one in his wrists. It wasn't entirely gone by noon, when Perla Pommeck appeared, wordlessly, eye severe, to deposit a tray on the floor near the door and immediately leave again. She locked the door, then returned to the apartment's largest room, in the middle of which Rathenau was studying a travel-sized chess board.

"So are you playing or what?" Perla huffed. "Make up your mind. What are you waiting for to give up that pawn?"

"I'm thinking," said Rathenau. "Be a pal and let me think, if you don't mind."

Perla sighed, inhaled, fell face forward like a chopped tree to the living room's dusty floor, and began a series of push-ups. Rathenau meditated, chin in hand, the other hand suspended above a pawn quaking for its life. Perla, meanwhile, pumped while counting aloud.

"Twenty-nine, thirty," she finished. "With the ones from this morning, that makes eighty. So are you keeping that fucking pawn or not?"

"All right," Rathenau conceded. "Anyway, there's nothing else I can do."

"Perfect," said Perla, jumping to her feet, then sliding her rook at top speed into a side road of the chessboard. "Too bad for your knight."

"Hm," Rathenau conceded. "I hadn't seen that. What's *he* up to, next door?"

"What do you think?" Perla said distractedly while plotting her next move. "So what time do we have to be at the hotel?"

As soon as Perla had left his room, Chopin approached the tray bearing a little food (an orange and some cold chicken) and a little reading matter (a slim, bound, dog-eared work, printed four-color and entitled *Better Living with Your Pet*). Once the latter was leafed through and the former eaten, he checked his pockets, which had not been emptied: neither his wallet nor his keys were missing, not even the passkey to the Parc Palace. Chopin felt relieved, though simultaneously a bit humiliated, that they hadn't removed his personal effects, as if they thought too little of him to apply these elementary precautions. To kill the time he reread his identity papers. Then he stationed himself at the window again, trying to identify the models of cars rushing in bits and pieces past the porthole in the soundproof wall: flashes of fugitive color, unreadable as blurry photos. He recognized not a one, save for a long, immaculate ambulance, tapered like a missile, headlights and warning beacons on full, hurtling down the highway shoulder.

Shirtless under his white smock with its upturned collar, a proud twenty-three-year-old West Indian was sportively piloting this ambulance. Next to him, lopsided on his seat, was Dr. Belsunce, whose divergent strabismus allowed for the double surveillance of both the traffic and the woman stretched out in the back of the emergency vehicle. Plaintive nasal whine and pinched lips, thin nose and very high forehead, a fragile melancholy in her eye, this woman, who looked more than a little like Blythe Danner, was complaining that she didn't feel too well, Doctor, that her head was spinning. The GP answered that it was nothing, Mrs. Belon, that it was entirely normal for her head to spin. At the clinic they'll see to that. Turn off that siren, Florimond, for God's sake, you can't hear yourself think.

The white Citroën CX continued to pass vehicles all the way to Porte d'Orléans, and from there it grafted itself onto the inner beltway, which it climbed the way a salmon heads up the Garonne River; the ambulance driver lost no occasion to sound the siren at top volume as far as Porte d'Auteuil. Having delivered the patient into the protective walls of the Roussel-Müller clinic, Belsunce then had himself taken back to the Parc Palace: it's really not necessary, Florimond, turn it off now. There's absolutely no call for that noise anymore.

Crossing the hotel terrace, the doctor shook several hands, minimizing a few symptoms that in passing they envisioned having him interepret for free. Reaching the lobby, he approached the reception desk at a sign from the concierge. The concierge was thin with a fine mustache; crossed gold keys adorned the lapels of his elegant mustard-colored outfit.

"I've got another woman out here who isn't feeling well," he announced. "She would like to see you."

"Very well," said Belsunce, "fine. In half an hour in my office."

Said office was furnished Empire-style and covered with vertically striped bronze-and-straw-colored wallpaper. Frames on the walls contained engravings, pastel portraits, and signed photographs of society ladies and oil barons. Watched over by old pharmaceutical jars (extracts of goatsbeard and mugwort, sassafras and senna), yards of bookbinding ran across the shelves to either side of the desk, on the surface of which an imitation-antique bowl contained a ragged red goosefeather, two top-of-the-line pens, and several souvenirs, among them an artificial hip fashioned into a mechanical pencil.

Having changed his bow tie, the doctor settled behind this desk to await his next patient, of which the archetype was a cackling, chattering, ring-laden wife, to whom he always prescribed the same powders. There was a knock and he got up to answer: black skirt and bolero, Suzy Clair did not match the standard description. "Well," Belsunce smiled kindly, "what seems to be the trouble?"

Faithful to his clinical technique, the doctor tried to appease his patient when she had related her sleeping difficulties: a bad night is just a bad night, to each his own rhythm, no rules in this domain, as many reactions as there are people. Did she get out a bit? It was good to get out a bit; conversation takes energy, after that you sleep much better. Did she play any sports? He spoke to her of the new swimming stroke he was trying to get right, a combination of the overarm with lateral kicks. And then she really should explore the surrounding area; one wouldn't think so but it's full of pretty sights—castles, for instance, still a few minor castles. He would lend her his Toyota if she liked. A good little car.

"In the meantime," he sniffed, scratching on his pad, "I'm going to prescribe a nice new compound. Or, actually, wait a moment, I must still have a few samples."

Rummaging protractedly in his drawer, he finally pulled out a light green packet, which he handed the young woman over the desk. "Here, try this. Start with a quarter pill at bedtime, and come back again if it doesn't work."

The telephone was in a state of solitary exasperation when Suzy returned to her room. At the other end, the general secretary apparently did not quite know how to introduce himelf.

"Veber. Vital Veber. Or Vital, if you prefer."

"Is there any news?" asked Suzy.

"Perhaps tomorrow," answered Veber. "By the way, the fellow who was bothering you, you know? You know who I mean? Well, he should leave you in peace from now on. He's left the hotel."

He hung up, smiling at the door that was just opening: Perla slipped her head through the crack. "Everything okay?" she asked.

Twenty-one

IN HIS TURN, at his slow pace, Mouezy-Eon rolled down the right-hand lane of the southern highway. A little before the Ville-juif exit, he parked his wheezing Renault R8 at the foot of the soundproof wall and pressed the hazard switch, triggering a *tutti* of blinking lights. Then he shut off the engine and searched in the glove compartment for one of those little statues that he sculpted in his off moments—in all sorts of materials, from bronze to bread dough—and that, typically, he was inordinately reluctant to exhibit, even in the discreet smoking parlor of the Parc Palace. This one, the size of a tin soldier, represented a man with a firm but supple expression, decisively erect on his pedestal: his thin lips and slightly hooded eyes fairly called to mind General Secretary Veber.

Mouezy-Eon examined his model for a few moments. With his thumbnail he gently inflected the overly hooked bridge of his subject's nose, then slipped the object into his pocket before laboriously extricating himself from the R8 by pushing on his back with one hand. He pulled a cable under the hood, which he left mouth agape. Then he walked around the vehicle and from the trunk took a red emergency triangle folded into a blue plastic pouch, unfolded it, and leaned it on its frail stand ten yards behind the R8. He proceeded slowly, wearily, holding shut the collar of his coat, consolidating the knot of his scarf, and having no thoughts at that moment but for his only son, a financial consultant in the process of divorcing in Laval: no telling if Jean-François would handle the separation well. Personally, Mouezy-Eon had never really gotten along with Jocelyne.

The cars sped close by, spattering him with their unfurling waves of cold air, dust, and whiny rumbling. Once the simulated breakdown had been properly staged, Mouezy-Eon began walking along the shoulder toward the porthole, in which, from the window of his jail, Chopin saw the old amateur painter's tired face appear several instants later.

After a brief hand signal, Mouezy-Eon rounded the phonic screen and crossed the weedy zone; the dampness made dark stalagmitic areas rise up his porous suede shoes. Avoiding the desolate garden-level apartments, he skirted the residence up to its main entrance before penetrating inside and calmly, casually going up the building stairs as if they were his own.

On the second floor, before anything else he had to make sure no one could witness what was about to happen. Mouezy-Eon rang without hesitation at the neighbors' across the hall, ready to show a gas worker's ID card, just checking for leaks, inspecting the pipes. But at three-something in the afternoon everyone was at work, school, or day care; the doorbell prompted nothing more than defiant chin movements from cats drunk on chopped kangaroo, dazed on their dirty kapok cushions.

Mouezy-Eon pulled the figurine from his pocket. Having examined it one last time, he shrugged his shoulders, then ripped off its right arm, which he remodeled in the form of a sausage. He introduced this little cylinder—a banal mixture of nitrocellulose and elastomer—into the keyhole and fitted it with a minuscule detonator. Then he had to try several times to make it catch: after two or three fizzles, the charge finally exploded with a furtive, incongruous noise, like a faulty muffler.

Once inside the apartment, the pre-retiree studied the locale, without particularly rushing to free Chopin. Gauging the state of the game abandoned midway, he cast a sympathetic glance at the black bishop's position, followed by another, more interested one at the reproductions of Eustache Le Sueur, Jacques-Charles de Bellange, and Lubin Baugin tacked to the living room walls. Half a dozen books also lay about on a fiberboard shelf: alongside some special issues of the magazine *Four Paws!,* he made out titles such as *I'm Training My Basset Hound, Great Danes and Mastiffs,* and *Everything But Speech.* The apartment seemed to have been deserted in a mad rush by a sect of eighteenth-century cynophilists at bay.

Before taking care of Chopin, Mouezy-Eon also sought out useful clues to the presence of Perla Pommeck and Rodion Rathenau—but except for remnants of sauce on a plate and of strategy on the chessboard, the couple had left nothing behind. All he had to do now was turn the key left in the keyhole: beyond the opened door, Chopin had just risen from his foam chair with an expression that was patient, resolved but distracted, ready for anything, as in a waiting room when it's about to be your turn.

"Where should I take you?" Mouezy-Eon asked after mutual greetings. "Would you like to rest awhile, or report directly to the colonel?"

"No," answered Chopin, "I'm going back to the hotel."

"That wouldn't be wise," noted the watercolorist. "You've been made there. The colonel wouldn't approve."

"I don't give a shit," Chopin testily summarized. "Let's go."

They left the apartment building and returned to the highway

by jumping the guardrails and rounding the soundproof wall, beyond which the incessant cars persisted in creating noisy drafts. As
they reached the flashing R 8, Chopin began shaking with cold. "I
don't give a shit about the colonel," he repeated. "There's something I have to do."

"As you wish," said Mouezy-Eon, who made sure to check the
oil before shutting the hood.

"And besides, I left my things at the hotel," Chopin argued as
he watched his finger tremble, "equipment I have to recover. It
wouldn't be too smart to let them find it, eh?"

"But *I* can take care of that," Mouezy-Eon emphasized as he
refolded his emergency triangle. "You're exhausted, it's plain to
see. Let someone else take over."

"No, no," Chopin's teeth chattered. "No."

They had gone, leaving the highway by the first exit ramp and
crossing a very homogenous stretch of suburb, perenially inhabited by the same density of people. Mouezy-Eon was still trying
to make Chopin see reason.

"If it's simply a matter of principle, there's no sense getting
all worked up over it. I know them, they'll find someone else to
handle it."

"That's not the point," admitted Chopin.

"Everything's the point," Mouezy-Eon reminded him. "So,
then, is it the young lady?"

Chopin didn't answer. The other said nothing, either.

"All right," he finally conceded, "I'll check with the doctor if
there's anything we can do."

"What," went Chopin, "Belsunce? He's in this, too?"

"What did you think?" asked Mouezy-Eon, pulling a local

daily from his pocket. "To tell the truth, he hasn't really been with us since last year; he found the Italians paid better. But it appears we can make arrangements with them these days." He held the paper out to Chopin. "Don't you want to see what's playing around here? It's better if no one saw you for a while."

So an hour later, Chopin found himself in blackness, the place where one can see you least, in the eighteenth row of the Pathé-Champigny. The film was titled *Paul* and it told the story of a young man named Paul who was very good-looking, but whom all the women abandoned, one after another. After his sixth serious breakup on the Pont Bir-Hakeim, in the rain, a disgusted Paul was emptying his bank account and renewing his passport when Chopin fell asleep. Two showings later, nails bloodied, two teeth missing, Paul was escaping from a prison in Jakarta when a hand shook Chopin's shoulder, causing him to open his eyes right onto the screen: at that moment, the unfortunate eponym was being skinned as he crawled under barbed wire, perspiration soaking his copper face. "Let's go," whispered Mouezy-Eon. Following the painter toward the cinema exit, Chopin looked back at the film: Paul had just taken a bullet in the shoulder blade.

There was blackness outside as well, and three steps were enough for them to dive into the ambulance parked in front of the movie house, curtains drawn. At the wheel, Fernandez now replaced Florimond. The ex-guardian of the expiatory chapel had donned the West Indian's white smock, naturally too large over his shirt, which remained regulation blue: the hems lapped over each other, the shoulders ballooned. "No sirens this time of night, of course, Fernandez," Mouezy-Eon recommended. "Just some revolving lights, in case."

"Won't he tell the colonel?" Chopin bravely whispered.

Mouezy-Eon shook his head. "This is on the side. No problem."

Approaching the hotel, Fernandez cut the lights. The CX avoided the main building and headed for the garages, where Dr. Belsunce's Toyota enjoyed the exclusive use of a lockup. Chopin got out of the ambulance, which immediately headed off. The doctor was waiting in the shadows, keys in hand.

"Good to see you again," he assured Chopin, pulling open the lockup door. "Here, you can make yourself comfortable over there."

He pressed a fat waterproof switch, causing a naked light-bulb to glare: alongside a set of snow tires, a removable baggage rack, and two cans of lubricant, some boxes of old books and old clothes were stacked in the back. Two African statuettes, a pair of wooden skis equipped with neolithic bindings. Then a standing closet with no door contained tied-up bundles of professional journals, virgin prescription pads, and several non-working tools in metal cases—dead sphygmomanometer and stethoscope, reflex hammers and tongue depressers, and rusted auricular, nasal, and rectal specula. Presence of a cask.

"No problem for the car this time of year," Belsunce informed him. "It can stay outside for a few nights."

As they arranged a corner for Chopin, the doctor told him of Suzy's visit the previous day, absolutely charming, I hadn't realized you two knew each other, I didn't know that. "Well, actually," said Chopin, "it's a bit complicated."

"She's in good health, in any case," Belsunce diagnosed. "A tad jittery, of course, needs to relax. I've lent her my car for tomorrow; I'll keep you informed. The blankets are over there. Obviously it's not exactly the Ritz, you won't be able to stand it for very long."

"I'm hoping to wrap this up quickly," Chopin ventured.

Twenty-two

AFTER ANOTHER more or less sleepless night, Suzy goes out to procure the sedatives prescribed by Dr. Belsunce. Having gotten up much too early, she leaves the hotel at around eight o'clock in the physician's Toyota.

The nearest shopping center is an esplanade ringed by sooty skyscrapers, between which floats a keen, insipid odor of plastic rot, not unlike the kind emitted by more than one supermarket. Far from enlivening the scene, the rare touches of color and vague ornamental sallies, which appeased, perhaps, the architect's conscience, only underscore the heaviness of the place, the way music sometimes increases a weighty silence instead of effacing it. With the same decorative intent, someone thought it pertinent to install a fountain in the middle of the paved walkway, a sort of modernist sphinx that relentlessly spews a narrow ribbon of flat water; and women skirt that fountain, loaded down with bags of provisions, and the men who follow them read their dailies as they walk, the pages opened directly to equestrianism or help wanted. All of them seem weary of confronting, or of no longer being able to confront, something—but this might be just an impression, Suzy reasons, it might just be me—except for the druggist, a short, efficient, lively man barred by a line of mustache, in full bloom on this humus rich in tranquilizing products.

After buying some for herself, Suzy leaves the pharmacy without a glance for either the sky or the buildings that define the sky. The towers stretch shadows in all directions, well beyond their reach. It is they that seem to have produced the waves of synthetic wind, the impersonal air currents that endlessly sweep the esplanade and make the tags dance above bins of produce, giblets, and fresh fish; they that disseminate the light objects trembling at ground level: odd tickets, crumpled wrappers, pages of yesterday's newspapers, bleached locks in front of the beauty parlor, dead leaves washed up from far away. Spotting a solitary playing card that had drifted there face down, Suzy refrains from turning it over with the toe of her shoe as if it were an old flat stone in some arid countryside, fearing the queen of spades as keenly as a nest of vipers. But she deciphers as best she can the texts of labels, the inscriptions painted on windows—gorgeous plaice, superb tuna, special on tongues and hearts—trying to divine the premises' modus operandi.

Leaving the shopping center, Suzy first crosses through other, analogous zones, massive rental complexes that crush pretty much everything in their path. Farther on, buildings with diverse functions stifle one another, mixed in with incessant scaffoldings that appear to threaten the entire sector by contagion. And so all this construction lives in a state of suspension, timid and resigned, hunched in anticipation of its downfall—even the most brilliant ceramic facade, squeezed between outmoded warehouses, seems sickly and withered in their shadow, victim of a judicial error.

As usual, the flanks of surviving buildings sometimes allow one to reconstitute the anatomy of those that have adhered to them: these great checkerboards composed of former kitchen, bedroom, or bathroom walls are a patchwork of alveoli, variously papered, paneled, tiled, or painted. Of the more or less tepid intimacies housed between these walls, then expropriated, there remains no more than this cutaway of inaccessible squares in waning colors, exposed to the cold and wind and public view, which Suzy deciphers while staring at them, recreating the biographies of insects. From ground level, one can make out the former placement of a double bed or sink, a water tank, a large oval frame; sometimes a perfectly intact soap dish remains caulked into the tiling of a bathroom, containing a relic of foamy drizzle.

Morning comes to the end of its role, lunches get their final touch-ups in the kitchen—last dabs of sauce in the wings, before the great vertical projector shines down on them. Suzy, having redonned her headphones in the car, is still listening to the same old soundtracks ("Would you care for some of my rabbit, Schumacher?"). She is in no great hurry to get back to the Parc Palace, lets herself be led by the car, abandons her initiative to it the way one relaxes a dog's leash or horse's reins and follows them in their meanderings, letting them pursue their own course but staying just vigilant enough to see that they don't bolt, don't bite anyone. Then, spotting a sign for Orly, she retakes control of the Toyota and sets a course for the airport. From among the different restaurants she will choose the most expensive, the most elevated; there she will eat alone while watching the airplanes take off.

Twenty-three

"SHE SHOULDN'T be long," said Belsunce, entering. "Did you manage to get some sleep? Everything's been taken care of. I've settled your bill and brought you this."

He shut the lockup door, put down Chopin's luggage, then handed a small paper bag to the entomologist, who was sitting on a chest with a horse blanket over his shoulders. Belsunce took a seat on a neighboring box, having first served himself a glass of wine from his cask. "You don't seem to be doing too well," his clinical sense judged. "You should have a little drink, while waiting."

"Thank you," Chopin sneezed, "I will." Then without appetite he opened the paper bag: a banana and more cold chicken; *I'm nothing but a chicken graveyard.*

Belsunce lifted the lid of his seat by one corner to remind himself of its contents, a fairly mildewed collection of *Physicians' Monthly;* from under the rope he extracted one of them and glanced over its table of contents while blowing off the dust. He seemed of a mind to spend a calm moment here, content with his glass in the hollow of his lockup as if in a club; content on his cardboard box as if in a club chair.

"I think I managed to catch a little cold, too," said Chopin.

"It's the season," Belsunce sagely pronounced. "I'll give you something for your stuffy nose, in just a moment."

Outside a fidgety wind had risen, fraying toward the lake's

horizon a band of clouds that released a few final droplets as they bolted, marking their territory under the hesitant sun.

A skeptical ray entered the room where Rodion Rathenau was resting. Stretched out on his bed, the bodyguard was rereading an adult espionage comic whose heroine was endowed with inconceivable charms. Rathenau was moved; the heels of his shoes nervously imprinted two dark crescents on the beige quilt. When the female spy tried to do all sorts of things to the male spy, Rathenau always imagined himself in the latter's place, Perla obviously playing in his reverie the role of the former—although she had always proved intractable on that score, pointing out in her brutal vocabulary that fucking on the job meant fucking up the job.

The room evidenced neglect. Everything in it more or less hung off something else: on the window latch, an unused hanger; two damp towels, pink and white, over the back of a chair, on top of which a half-closed suitcase lying crosswise spewed the sleeve of a long undershirt. The table, too, bore its load of crumpled magazines, empty cans in which cigarette butts exfoliated, and plastic liter bottles in which dregs went flat. Rathenau jumped when the door opened; rapidly he slapped the magazine over his groin.

"The idiot got away," Perla announced. "You should see what the door looks like. Somebody must have helped him. I was looking for you all over downstairs—what have you been up to?"

Imagining how to answer that, Rathenau first raked his throat.

"It really stinks in here," Perla sniffed. "Couldn't you let a little air in once in a while?"

As she crossed the room toward the window, Rathenau furtively adjusted his clothes before getting up, quietly slipping his reading matter under the bed. "Don't get so worked up," he said defensively. "Veber's at the cryptanalyst's, he's perfectly safe."

"Sometimes you can be so incredibly obtuse, B-12," deemed his colleague as she grabbed the phone.

"I told you to stop calling me that!" cried Rathenau.

At the cryptanalyst's, Vital Veber picked up immediately. The general secretary's voice connoted a glacial annoyance once Perla had explained the situation. "All right," he went. "Well, then, you're going to look for him now, do you understand? And then you're going to find him. Quickly. And then you'll bring him to me." Perla made a face, hung up without a word, and turned to Rathenau. "Come on," she said. "Get up. I've got an idea."

"A quarter to four," Dr. Belsunce noted in the meantime, closing a special issue on enterocolitis. "She's really taking her time. She's a sweet girl and all, but you know, *I* might need the car, too. I'll go see what she's doing."

"No," said Chopin, "I'll go."

"That wouldn't be very wise," Belsunce reflected.

"I don't give a shit," reiterated Chopin.

The physician was the first to leave the lockup, with Chopin hugging the walls a few yards behind. Occasionally, the other turned back to indicate with hand signals the coast's degree of clarity. Avoiding the main entrance, they advanced up to the terrace, from which one could reach the hotel restaurant, deserted at that time of day. From that point on, acting alone, avoiding the elevator, flattening every two minutes into doorways and corners, Chopin met only two bellboys in the stairway, absorbed in a technical polemic, and in the hallway of the fourth floor the sound of a footstep made him take brief refuge in the cleaning women's supply closet. When silence reigned anew, he headed toward Suzy's room, feeling deep in his pocket for the passkey. He unlocked the door, pushed it open, but had time only to notice the corner television (shut off) before being grabbed, pushed, and held in place by a very tight rear armlock, basically following the same procedure as the other night.

"You're becoming a pain, Chopin," Perla whispered into his neck. "This is getting boring. We're not going to keep playing this game over and over, are we? Huh?"

Chopin only hoped that they wouldn't inject him in the same spot as the night before last, but no, no shots this time: they just left the room, shoving him toward the elevator; Perla pressed the first-floor button. They got off without looking at each other, then Rathenau knocked twice loudly and three times softly on the cryptanalyst's door. Almost immediately, it was opened by Veber himself, a tan sheet of paper between his fingers, eye suspicious over his half-moon lenses. "Ah, right," he said. "Come in."

That day, the general secretary was wearing a houndstooth jacket over a pink shirt, with royal blue tie and trousers; an infinitesimal badge shone in the corner of his buttonhole like the eye of an insect. Behind him stretched a long table, at one end of which a fax machine whined. At the other end, as tall as and wider than a king-size sombrero, an imposing platter of shellfish stood by a long, fine-necked bottle of Tokay. Once the bodyguards framing Chopin had entered, a man who must have been the cryptanalyst disappeared into the next room, nabbing a shrimp as he went.

"One moment," said Veber.

He in turn left the room with his tan paper, returned with a white paper, slid it into a folder, then pulled a third document from the fax machine and read it, eyebrows knit; they had apparently come at a bad time. Then he removed his glasses and turned toward the newcomers, whom he pondered for a few moments, his look utterly detached, as if he were forcing himself to remember their identity, their nature, their means of reproduction, or even their hourly average or optimum cooking time. He finished by smiling imperceptibly, drawing a minute arabesque with the tip of his index finger.

"Perfect," he muttered. "Leave us."

The gorilla duo seemed disappointed. Rathenau was about to permit himself a cautious remark, but Perla touched his shoulder and they backed toward the door. "We'll be here," said Perla, "in the hallway. We'll stay here, just in case."

"Fine," said Veber, "fine. Or actually, no," he thought twice. "Better you took care of the young lady now. Bring her here, too."

Alone with Chopin, the general secretary afforded him the same brief and affectless glance that he had just given the documents: it was no comfort to feel oneself being leafed through like that, speed-read.

"Sit down," he then said. "Can I offer you something? A little wine, perhaps."

Paternal distraction, benign disinterest: the masters of the world act no differently when they receive the humble mailman and his urgent telegram in the kitchen. "Sit down," he repeated. Chopin sat while shaking his head, no thank you. "As you like," said Veber. Then a pause.

"I don't know what it is you do exactly in the intelligence business. A minor agent like so many others, I suppose. There are always a hundred like you wherever I go. You get used to it."

Another frozen glance, smile; another pause. Veber lifted an oyster from the middle of the platter, considered it much more tenderly, then set it back, terrified, among its peers.

"Normally I don't meet people like you," he resumed. "No time. Moreover, we let them do what they want, generally they're harmless. If there are problems, I have my security staff to deal with them. With you, it's a bit different. There's that young woman who, with whom…"

He trailed off, knitting his eyebrows once more, brushing aside his evocation of Suzy to develop the preceding point of his speech.

"If there are problems with people like you, there are two solutions, am I right? We can turn them around or we can eliminate them. Personally, I prefer turning them around. Although…" (An amusing memory flitted over his brow.) "What about you? Are you interested in working for us?"

"I don't think so," said Chopin. "Anyway, I'm only a technician."

Veber's smile increased a good dozen angstroms. A glowworm stirred in his eye.

"But that's just it. Exactly. In your field there are precedents, lots of precedents."

Chopin shrugged his shoulders; Veber smiled wider and wider, hysterically nearing a micron. "As far as Mrs. Clair is concerned," he added—but more knocks sounded on the door at that instant. "Well, I believe that's she."

Suzy appeared, dressed in the grey outfit she'd been wearing the day of the Shakespeare garden, alone. She looked at Chopin without seeming surprised, all this having to happen at some point. Immediately the general secretary began hovering around her, offering her a chair here, a drink there, apologizing for the inconvenience that the bodyguards must have caused her; he especially hoped she wouldn't hold it too much against them: by nature unpolished and devoted, but, alas, primitive, though fundamentally excellent beneath their coarse exteriors.

"No," said Suzy, "I came by myself. I didn't see them. But you were going to tell me, now," she continued in a voice with no illusions. "You promised me yesterday on the telephone. You must tell me where he is, now."

Veber hesitated, seemed to resign himself. Right. Chopin and Suzy watched him round the table near the mollusks and head for the partition door, open it, stick his head through the doorway. "It's all right," they heard him articulate, "you can come out." A pause, as usual, then the cryptanalyst appeared.

The cryptanalyst appeared, closed the door behind him, then leaned back against it while calmly gazing at those present. Suzy's eyes widened enormously. *Oswald,* her lips formed.

"There you go," whispered Veber, leaning toward Chopin. "Take Mr. Clair, for example. He's a precedent."

Then the silence remains heavy for a few instants, you bow under dozens of atmospheres, it's stifling, you find it hard to breathe; it's the ideal moment for the main door to open very suddenly, for the tall dark silhouette of Colonel Seck to appear in the entryway, clad in midnight blue as per usual. Squeezed in his powerful black fist, a chrome-plated Colt Diamondback shines in all its brilliance, the sole brightness in the half-light, the way a solitaire diamond glimmers on the fur of a femme fatale.

Twenty-four

"LET'S NOT WASTE any time," Colonel Seck smiled, his weapon aimed at the general secretary. "Let's get organized and proceed this way: Mr. Veber, you don't move. Chopin, you take Mrs. Clair for a walk on the grounds. Good. Now, Mr. Clair, you head for that door. Mr. Veber, you continue not to move a hair."

The colonel seemed relaxed, sure of himself. It seemed that nothing could spoil this perfect plan: Veber held still and Chopin approached Suzy, but Oswald Clair did not make a move, did not head for anything, which produced a gap in the perfect plan. The fax machine began whining in this gap: somewhere in the world, someone was launching a message across the ether in the direction of the Park Palace. Oswald Clair persisted in his immobility; the colonel continued to smile fixedly at him, his eyes soon clouding over with worried impatience, a bit like the face Titus makes when Berenice forgets her lines.

"Mr. Clair, you head—" he repeated in a more insistent and suspicious voice.

"I'm not heading anywhere," the cryptanalyst said calmly. "I want some guarantees first."

"Come now, Oswald," Veber smiled tenderly. "Since the man asked you."

His face brightening, he turned toward the colonel, who darkened at the same time, as if they had at their disposal but one smile for the two of them: a good, true smile, several centimeters long but oh so fickle, flitting carelessly from one to the other. For the moment, the bird was headed east.

"It would appear he doesn't want to," noted Veber. "Perhaps he'd like to stay. Perhaps even the young lady would like to stay, too. Who knows."

"The balance of power is on my side," the colonel pleaded, exasperated, "and don't forget it. If he doesn't come of his own free will, he'll have to come some other way."

"Where are his guarantees?" Veber questioned coldly. "What 'power' have you got, at the moment? You can't even be sure of the doctor. Who do you really have, aside from this amateur and the old painter?"

Chopin didn't react; he didn't mind the term *amateur* and found Veber to be really quite well informed. But the colonel hesitated; as he didn't know what to answer, the gap in his plan seemed to widen. Freeze-frame on the image: swayed by the prevailing wind from the east, the nearest tree branches regularly scrape the windowpanes, mimicking the sound of the projector motor. Then the door to the suite opened anew: this time it was Dr. Belsunce, harried, paternal, reassuring, as in the old days when he would spend the morning on his hospital rounds. His neutral eyes greeted everyone simultaneously.

"I came to see what was going on," he declared, "see if everything was all right. Is everything going your way, Colonel? Is the situation under control?"

"My word," went Seck, "I wouldn't say no to a little backup, perhaps. Would you be basically with me in this little affair, or basically not?"

Belsunce calculated rapidly. "I can't see any reason why not," he concluded, calmly drawing a Unique automatic from his vest pocket. The colonel relaxed. "Thank you, Doctor."

"Please don't mention it," said the physician while verifying the weapon's lateral safety. "Anyway, I couldn't refuse you this time, not after the Rappoport defection."

"I'm noting this, Belsunce," Veber said sourly.

His voice echoed tonelessly; his face froze. The volatile smile began to tire of him. With a flick of the wing, it crossed back through space: the colonel felt it touch down softly between the corners of his mouth, tenderly drawing them apart.

"All right," said Veber in a low voice, "let's negotiate. In certain conditions, it might be possible. I have recent and sensitive information, we'd have to see. Are you interested?"

"Personally, not very," answered the colonel. "But your idea will be a big hit with the surface committee."

He laughed, watching Veber blanch one shade lighter, then turned toward the cryptanalyst.

"And now, Mr. Clair," he said, lowering the barrel of his weapon, "you will put yourself in the doctor's hands. You may have all the guarantees you want. Otherwise, I will fire into one of your feet and you will be in the doctor's hands regardless. Good. Chopin, you take care of Veber."

"What with?" asked Chopin. "What do you expect me to take care of him with?"

"You mean you came unarmed?" Seck said indignantly. "You don't have anything on you? Goddammit, Chopin, are you a pro or not?"

"I'm just a technician," Chopin reminded him.

"Technician," the colonel repeated disdainfully. "But, I mean, look at Belsunce, at least he comes prepared. You wouldn't be carrying a spare, would you, Doctor? For Chopin?"

"Sorry," said Belsunce. "We'd have to go back to my place, and I don't believe we have the time. Naturally, if I had known…"

Exasperated, the colonel pulled a pair of handcuffs from his pocket and slapped them down next to the oysters. Take that, at least. Then he felt in his clothes, looking right next to his heart for a minuscule Kolibri with pink mother-of-pearl grip, which he grudgingly handed Chopin; his multiplied recommendations made it clear that he had a particular sentimental attachment to this weapon. It was a fond memory, you understand? A delicate little thing, and the trigger was ultrasensitive, so you had to be very careful. Be especially careful not to let it drop, of course, and then cock it *very* gently, without pulling too hard on the breech, otherwise it could play hell with the spring. Then it would be a whole big deal finding replacement parts for this particular model. Will that do?

Chopin pondered the extra-flat weapon with some embarrassment. Of course, you could kill people even with a .27, but even so, this didn't make him look very serious; it probably smelled like rice powder when fired. "It's pretty small," he said, "but all right. It'll do."

"Let's move," said Colonel Seck.

They left in the right order: Oswald Clair filed out in front of Belsunce, whose Unique embossed the right-hand pocket of his jacket; Suzy followed behind them; the colonel brought up the rear. Then Chopin turned toward Veber, who seemed worried, and spoke to him in a reassuring tone, with a nursely smile, as if it were a catheter and compresses he was brandishing instead of handcuffs and the Kolibri. "Well," he said, "I'm sorry, but I'm going to have to immobilize you. Come, let's have your wrists, please. Pull your sleeves up a bit, relax your arms, there you go. Perfect." Veber let himself be cuffed, his mind elsewhere, gravely preoccupied with the colonel's allusion to the surface committee and with the defection of his cryptanalyst—you might as well say his memory—not to mention the unforgivable absenteeism of his gorillas at such a time. The whole thing smelled a bit too end-of-career.

Several minutes later, when the bodyguards announced their presence via the agreed-upon code, Chopin placed himself behind the door, which he opened before slamming the Kolibri's grip down with all his might onto Rathenau's occipital bone. Despite his joy at seeing the hired hand immediately crumple, a mechanical scruple caused him to throw a quick glance at the little weapon, verifying that the blow hadn't too badly damaged the mother-of-pearl—an instant's inattention of which Perla took advantage to jump him.

If one sometimes has occasion to fight with the woman one loves, it's true that this occurs more rarely with the others; but the experience is no less unsettling. This violent female body set against him disturbed Chopin, dissipated his chances of winning all the more in that Perla battled very effectively, being much better trained in close combat than the average beloved. "Kill him, Perla!" Veber shrieked all the while. "Break his goddamned back!"

Rathenau had gotten up on all fours, massaging the back of his skull. Parrying as best he could, for an instant eluding Perla's clutches, Chopin managed vigorously to push the young woman back, causing her to stumble over her colleague and collapse on top of him—a bit too neatly, it seemed to Chopin as he fled through the still-open door.

"What the hell were you doing?" vociferated the general secretary, holding his bound wrists out to Rathenau.

"We were looking for the girl," Perla said, getting up. "You told us to go look for her, so we were looking."

"You're very bad," Veber bitterly stated. "You're really the worst. But I'm noting this," he repeated vehemently. "I'm noting everything. Get these off me, Rodion."

"Not right away," said Rathenau. "We're going to wait a bit."

"But . . . what's gotten into you, Rodion," said Veber, stiffening. "Have you gone insane? Would you kindly get these off me right now. Perla!"

"Calm down," said Perla, "calm down. Don't get so worked up. We're just going to wait for a tiny bit."

She walked over to the window, from where, through the branches, she could make out the little group that had just rounded the hotel toward the golf course, skirting the first bunker. As Chopin joined them at a run, she saw Colonel Seck instantly hold out his hand to reclaim his sentimental Kolibri.

The colonel minutely examined the little weapon, sniffed it, said yes, well, good enough. So you didn't need it after all? "Practically not at all," said Chopin. With rapid steps they crossed the close-shaven green toward the landing pier on the lake. They waited there less than a minute; Chopin looked at Suzy, the colonel at his Patek-Philippe, Belsunce at several things at the same time, and Suzy at the water and her husband, one after the other.

A hoarse rattle drifted in from the left, growing louder, taking shape in an outboard piloted by Mouezy-Eon. He maneuvered, drawing alongside the pier.

"Let's move," said Colonel Seck. "You three get on, quickly."

"Aren't you coming?" asked Chopin.

"No," answered the colonel. "From here on in, this no longer concerns me."

Suzy got on first, at the aft of the outboard; Oswald Clair took a seat next to her, and Chopin went astern, near Mouezy-Eon. The colonel immediately turned his back, but the doctor waved them good-bye when the motorboat started off toward the other side of the lake; then the two of them headed back up to the hotel. "You can go now," said Perla.

Rathenau undid Veber's handcuffs, saying, "Come on, let's go." They left the room; the general secretary entered the elevator seeming beaten, caved-in, vaguely wondering where he'd last seen the cyanide. They left the hotel, Veber following Perla and Rodion, who slowly walked down the terrace steps, stretching and relaxing as if at the end of a match. Belsunce, seeing them, jumped and moved a hand toward his weapon.

"Leave it," said the colonel. "Those two are mine now."

Twenty-five

THERE WASN'T ALWAYS a lake here. Once upon a time, there were great sandpits. Then they filled them with water, placed boats on top, and left a bit of sand so as to invent a beach; not far away they planted a robust mast in the water, bristling with diving boards, platforms, and metal ladders, looking like a derrick painted white. Next summer pedal boats will also float here, and windsurf boards glide, and paddlers blow. Every evening one of the boats, half submerged, will fill the role of high C in the grand finale of twilight, but we're not there yet. For the moment it's early spring, at the end of teatime, and the sky has cleared. Tightrope walker on the broken horizon line, the sun spills by vermilion bucketsful into the icy waters of the artificial lake.

During the crossing, Chopin did not turn around once, neither toward the Parc Palace nor toward the Clair couple quietly seated behind him. Piloting the outboard did not particularly suit Mouezy-Eon, who was not at all dressed for the occasion; moreover, his driving style was the same as behind the wheel of the R8, except that he steered the motorboat at breakneck speed, as if trying to be rid of it as fast as possible.

It was very rapidly, then, that they neared the opposite shore, where the recreational park gave the impression of a lawn neatly combed on the side, but victim of a violent growth spurt, tormented by the disproportion of its surface and ill at ease in this green suit that was too big, too new, like a well-bred young giant who doesn't know quite what to do with his body. No one frequented it at this hour during the week, except for three joggers following each other without looking, disappearing, reemerging to the rhythm of the shrub-lined undulations. Clean, monochromatic, and well ordered, this decor seemed as false as a painting or a transparency, the sole concrete relief being a very long black car parked on a steep incline not far from the shore—and the silhouette of a thin, dull man was immobile at water's edge, standing on a primitive berthing system, a fat iron ring sealed in a cement overhang.

Several yards from shore, Mouezy-Eon handed a coil of rope to Chopin, who tossed it toward the silhouette. The latter, leaning slantwise, took the rope, which it passed through the ring before underrunning the motorboat, then tossed it back to Chopin. Oswald Clair jumped to land before they had come to a complete stop, then moved off in hurried steps as if he knew the way, Suzy walking slightly behind him. Chopin wrapped the line around a cleat while watching them head toward the black automobile. Oswald turned back toward Suzy for a moment, uttered a few words while patting one of his jacket pockets; she answered with an icy smile that Chopin had never seen on her before. Mouezy-Eon shut off the engine.

"Let's go," he said, cautiously extricating himself from the outboard.

We who live in Western Europe very rarely see cars as large as that long black automobile; such models would obviously take up too much space on our little plots of land. One has to go search the vast expanses beyond the Atlantic or the Dnieper River to come across limousines of this format, which an elite labor force crafts with care on the assembly lines of Zil or Buick. On each of its flanks, three doors with smoked-glass windows opened onto three rows of pearl grey leather seats; short, sophisticated antennas attached to the rear fenders allowed one to receive all the radio signals in the world, and without much problem one could have held a dinner for thirteen around the hood. For his part, Chopin had never seen such a vehicle in the greater Paris region. He followed Mouezy-Eon in its direction, the bony silhouette dragging his leg a bit several yards behind them.

Nor had Chopin seen the man who was speaking with Oswald Clair through the lowered window, from his seat in the middle row. He was a frail-looking sexagenarian, drowning in a grey suit that blended with the tint of his seat, and seeming less settled than absorbed into this seat, from which only his face with its small, lively eyes and thin lips emerged. His fine hands also seemed to emerge from the seat, folded down like armrests and liable at any moment to be folded back up again. The yellow Gauloise that unfurled a line of grey smoke at the tips of his fingers thus seemed to be consuming itself, forgotten in the foldout ashtray at the end of the armrest.

When Chopin reached the car, followed by Mouezy-Eon and the silhouette, who immediately took his place at the wheel, Oswald Clair was pulling from his pocket a very small object, which he handed the man sitting inside.

"The important part is in there," he was saying. "Naturally, given the conditions, I wasn't able to take everything."

Chopin could not make out the exact shape of the object handed over by Suzy's husband, but it was really tiny, as small as the three walls of files the renegade had turned around six years earlier were thick.

"You managed to obtain the standards, I trust," said Maryland.

"All three versions," Clair confirmed, "with Ratine's amendments and the Boyadjian memorandum. You'll also find the minutes of the Technique and Forecast Group meeting, and most of their reports to the surface committee."

"The surface committee," Maryland wistfully mused. "If only I could get something on them."

"I've got their internal syntheses," said Clair. "For the past four years."

"What?" Maryland started. "They let you out with that, too?"

"Don't get your hopes up," said Clair. "They knew what they were doing. If it looks like I'm getting out with something substantial, it just helps them bury Veber a bit deeper. Outside the committee, no one knows that the information isn't particularly sensitive anymore. They'd been planning to modify their logistics for some time, anyway, so they don't really give a damn. The whole thing's of strictly relative value."

The three joggers reappeared, huffing and puffing like prehistoric horses; one of them wore a headband over his forehead, the other a Walkman over his ears, the third only his white shorts. Clair waited for them to move on before continuing:

"There's also the Jaspar file—does that ring a bell? I've got it."

"We already had that one," Maryland said modestly. "We've got that."

"The one you have is false. They passed it over with Morse, right?"

"Goodness, yes," said Maryland. "I believe it *was* Morse who..."

So wait. You're not saying that Morse…?"

Clair didn't answer.

"Good heavens," Maryland reflected, "little Morse. So he— And I who— Have you got any other names?"

"A few, and a couple more details besides. Some lists."

"That's fine," said Maryland, stubbing out his cigarette, "that's enough for now. We'll talk about all this in good time at the debriefing. Get in. Get in, all of you."

They divvied up the seats in the automobile: Suzy in front next to the driver, Chopin behind with Mouzy-Eon. Clair had settled next to Maryland, in the middle row, where they began reviewing the operation.

"So in the end," said Clair, "you get rid of the colonel into the bargain."

"He *was* a bit superfluous," admitted Maryland. "But it was mainly his choice, you see. He'd been wanting to leave for a while now."

"It makes me feel a bit funny to be swapped for him," Clair suddenly appeared moved. "I suppose he'll go back there with Veber. It would be something if they gave him Veber's job. Unless they're getting rid of him, too."

"They didn't so much swap you for Seck," specified Maryland, "as for Veber's liquidation. And the colonel will get by, don't you worry about him. I knew him in the fifties, at Patrice Lumumba University. He was getting by just fine even then."

The limousine crossed the suburban lands toward Paris; Chopin stopped listening to this dialogue of chiefs. Next to him, Mouezy-Eon was silent, having pulled a drawing pad from the folds of his beige coat and begun sketching little instant portraits of this or that view of the fleeting landscape. Chopin wondered how he managed to choose his subjects in this decor: in the apparent diversity of the suburbs, everything seemed affected with the same weight, the same taste; no form made any sense with any content; everything was hazy. In any case, Chopin was no longer looking at anything either, vaguely reflecting on his status as pawn, as bit player, nearsighted as a mole buried in the native soil. Finally, they reentered Paris.

On Rue de Rome, the mirror makers had just dumped a load of glass shards into a departing dump truck, which distributed a crepuscular kaleidoscope on the facades just as the black limo pulled up in front of Suzy's building. "See you tomorrow at the office," said Maryland to Clair. "And my respects and deepest thanks once again, Madam." She didn't answer. The couple dismounted without a single glance at anyone. "Left, Vito," said Maryland before turning back toward Chopin. "Where might we let you off?"

All along Boulevard de Courcelles up to Place des Ternes, Chopin premeditated what his evening would bring, standing alone by his window: a can of dinner and a little *Stilpon,* followed by the TV movie, Marianne bidding the entire country goodnight; then sooner or later one put oneself to bed. And the next morning the usual mail, the ads and the flyer, the postcard—ocean on one side, brief text on the other: *Wait for me. Suzy.*

"This'll do," he said. "You can drop me here."

FOR A FULL LIST OF PUBLICATIONS, VISIT:
www.dalkeyarchive.com

DAVID MARKSON, *Reader's Block.*
  Springer's Progress.
  Wittgenstein's Mistress.
CAROLE MASO, *AVA.*
LADISLAV MATEJKA AND KRYSTYNA POMORSKA, EDS.,
  *Readings in Russian Poetics: Formalist and Structuralist
  Views.*
HARRY MATHEWS,
  The Case of the Persevering Maltese: Collected Essays.
  Cigarettes.
  The Conversions.
  The Human Country: New and Collected Stories.
  The Journalist.
  Singular Pleasures.
  The Sinking of the Odradek Stadium.
  Tlooth.
  20 Lines a Day.
ROBERT L. MCLAUGHLIN, ED.,
  *Innovations: An Anthology of Modern &
  Contemporary Fiction.*
STEVEN MILLHAUSER, *The Barnum Museum.*
  In the Penny Arcade.
RALPH J. MILLS, JR., *Essays on Poetry.*
OLIVE MOORE, *Spleen.*
NICHOLAS MOSLEY, *Accident.*
  Assassins.
  Catastrophe Practice.
  Children of Darkness and Light.
  The Hesperides Tree.
  Hopeful Monsters.
  Imago Bird.
  Impossible Object.
  Inventing God.
  Judith.
  Natalie Natalia.
  Serpent.
  The Uses of Slime Mould: Essays of Four Decades.
WARREN F. MOTTE, JR.,
  Fables of the Novel: French Fiction since 1990.
  Oulipo: A Primer of Potential Literature.
YVES NAVARRE, *Our Share of Time.*
WILFRIDO D. NOLLEDO, *But for the Lovers.*
FLANN O'BRIEN, *At Swim-Two-Birds.*
  At War.
  The Best of Myles.
  The Dalkey Archive.
  Further Cuttings.
  The Hard Life.
  The Poor Mouth.
  The Third Policeman.
CLAUDE OLLIER, *The Mise-en-Scène.*
FERNANDO DEL PASO, *Palinuro of Mexico.*
ROBERT PINGET, *The Inquisitory.*
RAYMOND QUENEAU, *The Last Days.*
  Odile.
  Pierrot Mon Ami.
  Saint Glinglin.
ANN QUIN, *Berg.*
  Passages.
  Three.
  Tripticks.
ISHMAEL REED, *The Free-Lance Pallbearers.*
  The Last Days of Louisiana Red.
  Reckless Eyeballing.
  The Terrible Threes.
  The Terrible Twos.
  Yellow Back Radio Broke-Down.
JULIÁN RÍOS, *Poundemonium.*
AUGUSTO ROA BASTOS, *I the Supreme.*
JACQUES ROUBAUD, *The Great Fire of London.*
  Hortense in Exile.
  Hortense Is Abducted.
  The Plurality of Worlds of Lewis.
  The Princess Hoppy.
  Some Thing Black.
LEON S. ROUDIEZ, *French Fiction Revisited.*
LUIS RAFAEL SÁNCHEZ, *Macho Camacho's Beat.*
SEVERO SARDUY, *Cobra & Maitreya.*
NATHALIE SARRAUTE, *Do You Hear Them?*
  Martereau.
ARNO SCHMIDT, *Collected Stories.*
  Nobodaddy's Children.
CHRISTINE SCHUTT, *Nightwork.*
GAIL SCOTT, *My Paris.*
JUNE AKERS SEESE,
  Is This What Other Women Feel Too?
  What Waiting Really Means.
AURELIE SHEEHAN, *Jack Kerouac Is Pregnant.*
VIKTOR SHKLOVSKY,
  A Sentimental Journey: Memoirs 1917-1922.
  Theory of Prose.
  Third Factory.
  Zoo, or Letters Not about Love.
JOSEF ŠKVORECKÝ,
  The Engineer of Human Souls.
CLAUDE SIMON, *The Invitation.*
GILBERT SORRENTINO, *Aberration of Starlight.*
  Blue Pastoral.
  Crystal Vision.
  Imaginative Qualities of Actual Things.
  Mulligan Stew.
  Pack of Lies.
  The Sky Changes.
  Something Said.
  Splendide-Hôtel.
  Steelwork.
  Under the Shadow.
W. M. SPACKMAN, *The Complete Fiction.*
GERTRUDE STEIN, *Lucy Church Amiably.*
  The Making of Americans.
  A Novel of Thank You.
PIOTR SZEWC, *Annihilation.*
ESTHER TUSQUETS, *Stranded.*
DUBRAVKA UGRESIC, *Thank You for Not Reading.*
LUISA VALENZUELA, *He Who Searches.*
BORIS VIAN, *Heartsnatcher.*
PAUL WEST, *Words for a Deaf Daughter & Gala.*
CURTIS WHITE, *Memories of My Father Watching TV.*
  Monstrous Possibility.
  Requiem.
DIANE WILLIAMS, *Excitability: Selected Stories.*
  Romancer Erector.
DOUGLAS WOOLF, *Wall to Wall.*
  Ya! & John-Juan.
PHILIP WYLIE, *Generation of Vipers.*
MARGUERITE YOUNG, *Angel in the Forest.*
  Miss MacIntosh, My Darling.
REYOUNG, *Unbabbling.*
LOUIS ZUKOFSKY, *Collected Fiction.*
SCOTT ZWIREN, *God Head.*

FOR A FULL LIST OF PUBLICATIONS, VISIT:
www.dalkeyarchive.com